Enjoy all of these America

THE SILENT STRANGER

LADY MARGARET'S GHOST   A *Felicity* Mystery

THE TRAVELER'S TRICKS   A *Caroline* Mystery

SECRETS IN THE HILLS   A *Josefina* Mystery

THE RUNAWAY FRIEND   A *Kirsten* Mystery

THE HAUNTED OPERA   A *Marie-Grace* Mystery

THE CAMEO NECKLACE   A *Cécile* Mystery

SHADOWS ON SOCIETY HILL   An *Addy* Mystery

CLUE IN THE CASTLE TOWER   A *Samantha* Mystery

A GROWING SUSPICION   A *Rebecca* Mystery

MISSING GRACE   A *Kit* Mystery

CLUES IN THE SHADOWS   A *Molly* Mystery

LOST IN THE CITY   A *Julie* Mystery

and many more!

— A *Kit* MYSTERY —

INTRUDERS AT RIVERMEAD MANOR

by Kathryn Reiss

★ American Girl®

Special thanks to Judy Woodburn

Published by American Girl Publishing
Copyright © 2014 American Girl

Questions or comments? Call 1-800-845-0005, visit **americangirl.com**,
or write to Customer Service, American Girl, 8400 Fairway Place,
Middleton, WI 53562-0497.

Printed in China
14 15 16 17 18 19 20 LEO 10 9 8 7 6 5 4 3 2 1

All American Girl marks, American Girl Mysteries®, Kit®, Kit Kittredge®,
Ruthie™, and Ruthie Smithens™ are trademarks of American Girl.

This book is a work of fiction. Any similarity to real persons, living or dead,
is coincidental and not intended by American Girl. References to real events,
people, or places are used fictitiously. Other names, characters, places, and
incidents are the products of imagination.

The verses on pp. 102-104 are excerpted from the poem
"Little Orphant Annie" by James Whitcomb Riley, first published in 1885
under the title "The Elf Child."

PICTURE CREDITS
The following individuals and organizations have generously
given permission to reprint illustrations contained in "Looking Back":
pp. 174–175—courtesy of the Franklin D. Roosevelt Library and Museum,
Hyde Park, New York (orphans at table); Farm Security Administration–Office
of War Information Collection, Prints and Photographs Division, Library of
Congress, LC-USW36-748 (girl in pink dress); pp. 176–177—courtesy of the Ohio
Historical Society (Harriet Beecher Stowe house, tunnel); North Wind Picture
Archives (escaping slave); pp. 178–179—courtesy of the National Underground
Railroad Freedom Center (interior of safe house); courtesy of the Ohio Historical
Society (Harriet Scroggins Brown); Library of Congress, Prints and Photographs
Division, LC-USZC2-5399 (poster); © Corbis (soup kitchen); pp. 180–181—cour-
tesy of the Franklin D. Roosevelt Library and Museum, Hyde Park, New York
(Thanksgiving at orphanage); Amazing Stories name is a Registered Trademark
owned by Steve Davidson & The Experimenter Publishing Company (magazine
covers); p. 182—Used with the acknowledgement of the Frank R. Paul estate, and
approved by his great-granddaughter, Eliza (illustration of the future).

Illustrations by Sergio Giovine

Cataloging-in-Publication data
available from the Library of Congress

*This book is dedicated with love to
our two youngest children,
Dolores and Raymond—
brave adventurers both.*

*And special thanks to Louise Reiss
for the yummy description of
Cincinnati chili*

TABLE OF CONTENTS

1
A CRY FOR HELP

Kit Kittredge hurried along the sidewalk, feet crunching crisp autumn leaves. It was early October, and the trees were a blaze of color. Smoke curled from the chimneys of some of the grand houses in Uncle Hendrick's neighborhood. Her own house, Kit knew, would have a cheerful fire as her mother prepared the evening meal for the boarders who lived there, but Uncle Hendrick's house was never cheerful.

Kit sighed, hitching her schoolbag onto her shoulder. Last month, when Uncle Hendrick had complained that his arthritis was worse and he needed someone to look after him, he had asked for Kit. Mrs. Kittredge pointed out that there were plenty of women desperate for work these days. She suggested he hire one to help out until he felt better. But Uncle Hendrick had hired Kit to help out before, and he said she got the job done. Kit was happy to have the job, even though her great-uncle was often grumpy and his elegant house always felt cold.

So now, Kit walked to Uncle Hendrick's house after school several days a week and came home two hours later with the coins he paid her for her work. She was pleased to hand the money over to Mother. Times were hard, and money was scarce. Kit's family had nearly become homeless when her father lost his job. Their decision to turn their home into a boarding house had kept them going. For the past two years there had been lodgers to feed, rooms to clean, and extra laundry to do, but the whole family pulled together. Kit's father worked part-time at the airport now. The rest of the time he helped with the boarding house. Kit's older brother, Charlie, sent money home from Montana, where he worked for the National Park Service.

Wealthy Uncle Hendrick, who had never approved of Kit's family's taking in boarders, didn't understand about being poor. The gracious old homes in his neighborhood were large and elegant. There were hardly any signs of the Depression on Uncle Hendrick's street at all, Kit thought. Except for the house next door to his.

Kit stopped at that house as she always did and peered through the wrought-iron gate. When the afternoon sun hit the colorful panes of glass in the center window, the glass glinted like a large eye, winking. But aside from the pretty window, the house did not look inviting at all. The tall boxwood hedge around the property was overgrown. The lawn was full of weeds. The vegetable patch was tangled. The brick house seemed like a once-grand lady whose gown had faded. This house looked as if it understood about the Great Depression, Kit thought.

She started walking again, then stopped short. *What was that sound?* There—it came again. A mewing cry. Could a kitten be lost in the tangles of the overgrown garden?

Over a year ago, Kit had taken in a stray dog—a large basset hound that she named Grace. Grace had been homeless and sad, but she soon became a loved and pampered pet. If Kit found a homeless kitten now, would Mother let her keep it?

Kit moved back to the gate. "Here, kitty, kitty!" she called. The quavering cry came again, louder now, and this time it sounded less like a cat and more like a human.

"Hello?" called Kit.

A weak voice answered, "Help! Over here!"

Kit fumbled to lift the latch. She pushed hard to swing the gate open. The voice called again, sounding even weaker. She followed the voice across the grass to the hedge, and then gasped at what she saw.

An elderly woman lay sprawled on the grass, one leg twisted beneath her. "Oh dear!" exclaimed Kit, kneeling to help the woman sit up. The woman's white hair straggled out of its bun, and her watery blue eyes blinked at Kit.

She reached out a hand and groped in the

grass. Kit found her spectacles lying just inches away. The woman smiled gratefully and set the spectacles on her nose.

"Thank you," the woman said. "It's my ankle. I've turned it. If you hadn't heard me calling, I'd probably have lain here all night until the postman came tomorrow." Then she murmured something under her breath, something Kit could barely hear: "Or until one of the travelers found me . . ."

"Travelers?" asked Kit. "Do you mean hobos?" Homeless people sometimes went through nice neighborhoods asking for work. One of them might have assisted this old woman if Kit had not heard her.

The woman shook her head and smiled faintly. "No, not hobos. But never mind. You've found me, and I'm safe now. So tell me who you are, and how you happened to be passing by just when I needed rescuing!"

"I'm Kit Kittredge. And I'm on my way to my uncle's house next door. He's my great-uncle, actually. My mother's uncle."

The woman peered at Kit. "Oh! Then you're the one I've seen sweeping his front steps and hanging out his laundry. A hardworking girl." Her blue eyes narrowed. "I'll wager the old codger's paying you less than half of what you're worth. He's a skinflint! Always has been!" Then she smiled at Kit again and held out one thin hand. "Very pleased to meet you, dear girl. I'm Miss Elsie Mundis of Rivermead Manor."

Kit shook her hand. "Pleased to meet you. Now, shall I help you into the house?"

"I'd be much obliged."

Leaning heavily on Kit, Miss Mundis was able to get to her feet. She took Kit's arm and limped to the house.

Kit helped Miss Mundis through the front door and looked around eagerly. Inside, a chandelier hung from the hallway ceiling. There was a faded Oriental rug on the floor, and a curving staircase leading upstairs. Miss Mundis limped down the hallway into a sunny kitchen.

A china cup and saucer and a teapot sat on the round kitchen table. A shabby armchair by the windows held a fat white cat. Kit glanced at the magazine on the table: *Amazing Stories.* The curtains at the windows were faded, and the kitchen floor was in need of a good washing, but the room had a homey air. Kit thought that Miss Mundis probably spent a lot of her time here.

Miss Mundis sank into the armchair with a sigh of relief. She settled her cat on her lap.

"Where were you when I needed help?" she asked the cat. "Snoozing in the sun!" She smiled at Kit. "Stanley's a lovely companion, but not very useful in an emergency."

Kit laughed and reached out a hand to stroke Stanley's soft fur. "I have a dog named Grace."

"How nice," said Miss Mundis. Her voice was cheerful, but Kit noticed that Miss Mundis winced as she shifted in her chair.

Kit saw a telephone on the wall by the icebox. "Do you want me to call your doctor?"

"There's no need. I'm sure I shall be fine. But I'm wondering if you could manage a second job. Perhaps you could work for me on the same days you come to your uncle's house."

"I'd love to," said Kit eagerly. "I'd have to ask my parents, of course, but as long as I get home for dinner, I'm sure they won't mind."

"I'll pay you, of course," Miss Mundis added. "Probably more than your skinflint uncle does! I need help with the sweeping and dusting, and perhaps you can make something simple for my supper. It's hard for me to keep up with things as I get older."

"So you live here alone?" asked Kit. "With Stanley, of course."

Miss Mundis darted quick glances around the kitchen as if someone might be waiting in the shadowy corners. "I'm not alone anymore," she whispered, and her eyes sparkled as if she were in possession of a special secret.

Curious, Kit was about to ask Miss Mundis what she meant when she abruptly changed the subject, asking if Kit could start work that very week.

"I'm sure my parents will say I can," Kit said. "But why not let me help today, since I'm here now?" She smiled at Miss Mundis, who sat stroking her large white cat with a trembling hand. "I could make you some sandwiches before I go, like I do for Uncle Hendrick."

"Sandwiches would be lovely, dear, and perhaps a cup of tea, too?" As Kit set water on to boil for tea, Miss Mundis picked up a penny that lay on the table and flicked it into the air. "Heads I'll have cheese, and tails ham—how is that? Oh, bother!" They watched as the coin hit the floorboards, spun around twice, and then disappeared down a crack.

"So much for gambling, eh, Kit?" Miss Mundis chuckled. "That penny's down in the cellar now. Well, cheese or ham, it's all the same to me. Just don't use up all my provisions in case someone else should need something to eat . . ."

Kit chopped cheese and onions together to make a sandwich filling. As she worked, she pictured a whole stash of coins piled in the cellar beneath the kitchen floorboards, like a pirate's treasure.

"I'm so grateful for your help," Miss Mundis said as Kit served the sandwiches.

"You're sure you don't want me to call the doctor?" Kit asked, pouring out a cup of tea for the old woman.

"I'll be fine, dear. If there's trouble, I'll call on my time travelers."

"Time travelers?" repeated Kit, puzzled.

But Miss Mundis shook her head. "Oh, don't mind me," she said with a little laugh. "Your uncle would just say I read too many science fiction novels!"

Then she insisted on limping to the front door to show Kit out. "I will look forward to seeing you again soon," she said, and shut the heavy wooden door firmly.

2
A DESPERATE WOMAN

Kit walked to her uncle's house next door and let herself in. She could hear him talking to someone, and she followed the sound into the kitchen, where he stood at the back door, frowning down at a bedraggled woman on the step. Uncle Hendrick's little black Scotty, Inky, growled at Uncle Hendrick's side.

"Please!" Kit heard the woman cry. "I need work desperately."

Uncle Hendrick's voice was brisk. "Mrs. Addison, I don't need a housekeeper. You've been a laundress in this neighborhood for many years, so I'm sure your employers will continue to have clothes for you to wash."

"But I told you—I've lost everything!" The woman spoke through her tears. "How can

I take in laundry when I don't have a home to work from?"

Uncle Hendrick motioned for Mrs. Addison to leave, but she did not go. Her husband had gone off to New York in search of work, she explained. She hadn't heard from him in a year. Her landlord had put her out in the street because she couldn't pay the rent. "And now," she said, her voice breaking, "I've had to take my five children to the orphanage because I couldn't care for them while looking for work."

"Well, that's fine," replied Uncle Hendrick calmly. "Now they will be cared for."

"Oh! What is to become of us?" She gasped for breath.

"Get a hold of yourself, Mrs. Addison. I have household help already. Please pull yourself together, madam, and be on your way!"

Inky yapped as if in agreement. Then he saw Kit and ran, barking, to her side.

"Why, here's my help now," Uncle Hendrick said.

Weeping, Mrs. Addison looked past him to

Kit and shook her head. "A child can't do all the work of a household! Please, I beg you—"

Kit's heart sank as Uncle Hendrick's scowl deepened. "You will find work elsewhere," he said firmly. "Good-bye."

"Yes—I'll be on my way." Mrs. Addison drew a deep breath and glared at him. "Heaven only knows when I'll ever see my babies again."

Kit watched with shocked eyes as Mrs. Addison hurried off down the driveway.

Uncle Hendrick turned to Kit. "You're late, girl," he said mildly. "But I'm glad to see it's you and not another hobo asking for work. I've had four of them stop by already this week, as well as a self-righteous man asking me to turn my home into a boarding house!" He shook his head in disgust. "Another do-gooder. Your parents take in boarders for money, but I don't need money, so why would I take in riffraff off the streets?" Uncle Hendrick strode inside, muttering under his breath.

Kit hurried behind him. "Sorry I'm late," she

said, "but your neighbor, Miss Mundis, fell and needed help."

Uncle Hendrick turned to look at Kit. "Elsie Mundis? Was she badly hurt?"

"No, I don't think so," Kit replied. "She twisted her leg and had a hard time getting to her feet. But once she was inside the house, she seemed all right."

"She'll be fine. That old biddy's perfectly healthy, even if she's crazy as a loon. We went to school together, and she was muddleheaded then, too. Always had her nose stuck in a penny dreadful—ludicrous novels about rockets to the moon and Martian attacks! Distant galaxies and little green men! Couldn't have two minutes of conversation with her before she'd give you one of her silly stories to read." He sat down heavily at the kitchen table. "Impossible woman!"

"She seems nice," ventured Kit. She set to work scrambling eggs for Uncle Hendrick's supper. There was the meal to make, the parlor to dust, and Inky to walk around the block before she could head home.

"Help out if you like, but don't listen to a word Elsie Mundis says," Uncle Hendrick counseled, as Kit dished up a mound of fluffy eggs. "If you do, you'll soon be as barmy as she is!" He opened his newspaper, but Kit soon heard him muttering under his breath. "If I'd known she needed help, I could have sent that lady hobo."

"What a good idea!" Kit turned from washing up the dishes and smiled. "I don't need the job as much as Mrs. Addison does."

"She'll have moved on," Uncle Hendrick replied. "I wouldn't know where to find her even if I wanted to." He snapped his paper decisively. "And don't you go looking for her."

Kit didn't know where to look for Mrs. Addison, either, but she made up her mind she would keep an eye out for her.

Kit finished her chores, dragged an unwilling Inky around the block, then said good-bye to Uncle Hendrick. As she hurried out his door, shiny coins clutched in her hand, she couldn't help feeling excited about her new job at Rivermead Manor. There was certainly something odd about the place—and about Miss Mundis. She had never explained what she meant about time travelers. Did she mean people from the future—or the past—coming to *now*?

That, of course, was just plain impossible. Still, as she passed the gate of Rivermead, Kit looked uneasily at the long shadows of the trees and at the manor house's single lighted window. Then she dashed down the street toward home.

3

THE UNDERGROUND RAILROAD

"There you are, Kit." Mrs. Kittredge, her face flushed from the warmth of the stove, reached out to squeeze Kit's shoulders in a quick hug. "Mrs. Howard is in bed with a terrible cough, so I've been short a pair of hands—just when we have a new boarder!"

Kit put her schoolbag in the corner of the kitchen and hung her coat on a hook. She tied an apron behind her back. "Who is it?" she asked.

"His name is Mr. West, and he's just arrived. I've put him in with Mr. Peck. He's—" She broke off, shaking her head. "Here, dear, will you take these bowls to the table? Everyone will be down in just a minute. Then you'll meet the gentleman for yourself."

Kit pushed through the swinging door into the dining room, where several of their lodgers were already assembled.

Mismatched chairs were pulled up to the long dining room table. Mr. Peck was already seated. He was a friendly man who sometimes entertained them all by playing his double bass. Miss Hart and Miss Finney, two nurses just home from their long shifts at the hospital, settled into their places. Beside them was Mr. Bell, an out-of-work actor who spent his days cleaning windows now. Kit's friend Stirling Howard sat across from Mr. Peck. The chair where his mother usually sat remained empty as the room filled with the hungry boarders. There was no sign of the new Mr. West.

Mrs. Kittredge entered with a tureen of fragrant vegetable soup. "Will you dish up?" she asked Kit. "I'm going to prepare a tray to take up to poor Mrs. Howard."

As Kit was ladling out bowls of soup, her father passed bread, applesauce, and the heavy teapot. Just as everyone began eating, a tall, middle-aged man with a shock of graying hair appeared in the doorway. In one hand he carried a notebook, in the other a pencil.

"Good evening, Mr. West," said Kit's father. "Everyone, please welcome Reginald West."

Mr. West nodded from the doorway. "So this is how it's done," he said genially. "Dinner at a boarding house." He flipped open his notebook and jotted something with his pencil. "And what's on the menu? Soup?" He made another notation. "Very nice. Economical and filling."

Mr. Kittredge motioned to the empty chair next to Stirling. "Sit here for now, Mr. West."

"Ah," said Mr. West, sitting down. "Enough chairs need to be found for all the boarders." He made another note.

Kit watched him curiously. She wanted to be a reporter when she grew up, and she often made notes in notebooks, though Mother would frown on such behavior at the dinner table.

Mrs. Kittredge returned to the room with the news that Mrs. Howard was resting comfortably. As everyone started talking about their day, Kit watched Mr. West. Every now and then he jotted something in his notebook.

"You are to be commended, Mr. and Mrs. Kittredge," he said when he'd finished his soup. "You are providing nourishing food and a clean place to lay our heads during these hard times—even though it means your home is no longer your own. We salute your generosity!"

The other boarders looked surprised at this little speech, but nodded their agreement. "Hear, hear," said Mr. Peck, applauding lightly. Under the table, Grace thumped her tail hard. Everyone laughed.

But Mr. West looked serious. "There are many homeowners in town who might also open their homes, but choose not to."

"We feel lucky to have you all," Mrs. Kittredge said. "Running a boarding house is how we keep our home."

"There are plenty of large homes in the wealthiest areas of town that could shelter local homeless people," Mr. West said, frowning. "But do those people open their homes? No!

In the name of public service, they should!"

"He makes a good point," Miss Finney murmured to Miss Hart.

Kit thought about Uncle Hendrick's large home, with only him living there. She thought about Miss Mundis, alone at Rivermead Manor.

"Are you a Communist?" asked Mr. Bell, frowning.

"Indeed I am not!" protested Mr. West. "But I believe in sharing good fortune. Rich people in big houses should help hardworking people down on their luck." He patted his notebook. "I may write up my idea for the newspaper. A plan to get more boarding houses up and running in our city."

"I've heard of parents putting children into orphanages because they can't keep a roof over their heads," Mr. Peck said, and Kit remembered poor Mrs. Addison.

Miss Hart spoke softly. "Times are so hard that even the soup kitchens don't have enough food."

"Better to light a candle than curse the

darkness," Mr. West said passionately. "To get housing for people in need, I've begun canvassing the entire city of Cincinnati, starting with the wealthier neighborhoods. If enough homeowners rented out rooms cheaply, we could get many more people fed and housed." Mr. West flipped a page in his notebook and wrote furiously. "Simple as that."

❧

During school the next day, Kit's class walked to the public library for a special presentation. "Pay close attention," their teacher, Mr. Leiser, told them as they entered the building. "You will be responsible for group presentations about what you've learned today."

The librarian, Mrs. Newcomb, greeted Kit's class and invited them to sit in the chairs arranged in rows in the children's room. Kit sat in the first row next to her good friend Ruthie Smithens and watched as children from other schools filed into the large room. She noticed that one was a class of colored children. They sat at the back. Kit's eyes widened as she recognized one of the girls. Jessamine Porter! She'd known Jessamine when they were little. Jessamine's father had worked for Kit's father's dealership before Mr. Kittredge lost his business.

Kit turned in her seat and waved to catch Jessamine's eye. Jessamine looked up and saw Kit. With a leap of happiness in her eyes, Jessamine raised her hand to wave back.

"Who's that?" whispered Ruthie, and Kit quietly told her.

"We used to play together," Kit said. "My father let us sit in the new cars, and we had such fun pretending to go on journeys."

"I never had a colored friend," Ruthie whispered, peeking over her shoulder at Jessamine.

Kit glanced back at Jessamine, too, and saw that the other girl was looking right at them. Kit grinned at her and moved her hands as if driving a car. Jessamine giggled and quickly put her hands over her mouth. Kit hastily turned around again before Mr. Leiser could scold her.

She murmured to Ruthie, "Jessamine's nice. We played on the weekends. Her father worked on the cars. Sometimes he would push us on the big tire swing that Dad hung behind the shop."

Mrs. Newcomb welcomed her audience. "Has anyone heard of the Underground Railroad?" she asked.

Stirling's hand shot up. He spoke with assurance. "It wasn't a real train," he explained. "It was a way people escaped slavery. Back in the time of slavery, Ohio was a free state, and Kentucky, to the south of us, was a slave state. Lots of escaping slaves came through Cincinnati because it was right on the border."

Kit smiled. Before the Howards came to live at Kit's house, Stirling's mother had worried a lot about his health. She'd kept him indoors, and he'd spent a lot of time reading. The things he'd learned made him one of the smartest pupils in class.

"Thank you, Stirling, that's correct," said Mrs. Newcomb. "Escaping slaves would come across the Ohio River and find shelter here for a night or two until they could move on. The people who opposed slavery were called abolitionists. And the whole secret enterprise of people moving along, stop by stop, to freedom in the North was called the Underground Railroad."

Kit listened intently. Could her own house have been part of the Underground Railroad? No—her house was too new.

There must be a lot of people who didn't know about the part Cincinnati had played in helping slaves escape to freedom, Kit thought. This topic might make a good newspaper article. The editor of the paper had said that when Kit wrote something good enough to print, he'd print it. Once she'd had a letter to the editor published, and a couple columns on the children's page. She wanted her next story to be printed in the main section of the newspaper, the part with important news.

Kit listened closely as Mrs. Newcomb told the students about Harriet Beecher Stowe, whose novel, *Uncle Tom's Cabin*, brought to life the misery of slavery. Harriet Beecher Stowe had come from a whole family of abolitionists. Slaves on the run had found shelter in her house. But hers was only one of several homes in Cincinnati that had been stations on the Underground Railroad. Some homes were even rumored to have secret hiding places. "Besides the Stowe house," said Mrs. Newcomb, "there were the Wilson house and Rivermead Manor, among others."

Kit caught her breath. Rivermead! That was Miss Mundis's house! She could interview Miss Mundis for her newspaper article.

Then Mrs. Newcomb read them a dramatic folk story about slaves using the stars to find their way north to freedom. Kit listened carefully in case the information might be useful for her article. She noticed that Ruthie was listening attentively, too.

When the librarian finished, all the children applauded. Then Kit hurried over to speak to Jessamine.

"Hi, Jess!"

"Hello, Kit. I almost didn't recognize you."

"I'm not so different—just taller. You're a lot taller, too." Kit and Jessamine looked at each other, and Kit suddenly felt shy. But Jessamine seemed pleased to see her.

"Which school do you go to?" Kit asked.

"I'm in a new school now."

"Is it near here?" Kit asked.

Jessamine pointed down the street. "It's that way, all the way past the railroad tracks."

"Oh!" Kit said. "I think if you turn and go up the hill instead of crossing the tracks, that's where my Uncle Hendrick lives."

"Right . . ." said Jessamine slowly. "I know what neighborhood you mean."

"So where do you live now?" Kit asked.

Jessamine busied herself with her jacket as if she hadn't heard Kit. The teachers were lining their classes up, and Kit knew she had only a minute before they'd leave the library.

"It's nice to find you again," Kit said. "Maybe sometime we could . . ." But they couldn't really play in the cars anymore, or swing on the tire, and white children didn't usually play with black children in their city. But . . . *why shouldn't we see each other sometime?* thought Kit.

"Where do you live?" she asked Jessamine again.

"We've got a long walk back to school now," Jessamine said abruptly, not meeting Kit's eyes. "Good-bye." She moved away.

"Wait!" Kit called.

Mr. Leiser motioned Kit into line. As they walked back to school, Kit told Ruthie how Jessamine had turned away. How Jessamine wouldn't tell her where she lived.

"She was always so nice," Kit said sadly. "I thought she'd *want* to play together again."

"Well, isn't it obvious?" asked Ruthie.

Kit raised her eyebrows. "What?"

"Well, your father lost his business. So her father lost his job, too."

Kit nodded slowly. "You're right. We were able to keep our home by taking in boarders, but maybe Jessamine's family lost their home." Her heart felt heavy. Were the Porters living in a hobo shack down by the train tracks?

Kit decided she would ask her parents if there was any way to help Jessamine's family. If only there were more rooms in Kit's house! But . . . would a colored family move into a white family's boarding house?

Kit didn't think so. She remembered how Jessamine's class had sat at the back of the semi-circle in the library, even though they had not been the last to arrive. There were no black children in Kit's class, and there were no white children in Jessamine's class.

For a second, an image like a moving picture flickered in Kit's mind—of two girls hanging together on a tire swing, flying through the air, shrieking with laughter. It seemed to Kit that it should be a simple thing to be friends with Jessamine, but she realized it was not.

❧

As they walked home after school, Kit, Ruthie, and Stirling discussed what sort of presentation to do for their class assignment. Kit suggested their group write a report about the local homes that were part of the Underground Railroad. They could start by talking to Miss Mundis! Maybe she had some historical records packed away.

"There's nothing I'd like better," Kit said, "than reading an old diary left by an escaping slave. Wouldn't that make an amazing primary source for my newspaper article? Mr. Gibbs at the newspaper always says that primary sources are better than gold to a reporter!"

"Well, I don't think most slaves could write," said Stirling. "They weren't allowed to learn."

Ruthie said she'd rather do a play of the folk-tale Mrs. Newcomb had told them.

"But that's not real," Kit protested.

"Well, it's more interesting than writing an old report," Ruthie responded. "If we put on a skit, we can have costumes and props and maybe even special light effects!"

"Well, what if you play Harriet Beecher Stowe, and Kit plays a reporter interviewing you?" suggested Stirling as a compromise. "That's factual, but you'd still get to wear old-time costumes."

"Good idea," Kit said. "And you could play the photographer," she told Stirling.

Kit left Ruthie and Stirling discussing how to stage the skit and hurried along on her way to Rivermead Manor.

4

THE TIME PORTAL

Kit knocked on the front door of Rivermead Manor. Through the colored glass she could see Miss Mundis limping down the hallway.

Miss Mundis greeted Kit with a weak smile. "Oh, good! I thought you might be that man again."

"What man?" Kit offered Miss Mundis her arm to lean on as they walked to the kitchen.

"He came last week and again today, trying to convince me to turn Rivermead into a boarding house! The fellow believes it is the civic duty of people with big houses to provide low-cost places for the homeless." She sighed, looking around her large kitchen. "Maybe he's right. But I just don't have the strength on my own."

"We have a new boarder at our house who was just talking about that same thing."

"Oh, I didn't realize your family took in boarders."

"We had to—after my father lost his business."

"Well, bless your heart." Miss Mundis pursed her lips. "I believe the man who came here told me his name was Mr. West. He's a tall, gray-haired fellow."

"That's our new boarder!" said Kit.

"Your mother has her hands full, then," Miss Mundis chortled. "Now here's an idea. I'll take in lodgers who pay their rent in home repairs! Something always needs doing around here. Lightbulbs are always burning out, and now I can't get to the store for new ones. There's a water pipe leaking in the cellar, and it's left a puddle of water on the floor. This old house will be the death of me!" She shook her head. "I wish I had the money to hire a handyman. But I'm sure you'll be a great help."

"Well, I'll mop up the water in the cellar for

you," Kit offered, a bit hesitantly. "But I don't know how to fix pipes . . ."

"Now don't you worry. I've lived here since I was born, and I'm sure I'll find a way to keep the house holding up for the next generation. This house has quite a history, you know. My ancestor, Edgar Mundis, built Rivermead over a hundred years ago, and it was part of the Underground Railroad."

Kit seized this opening. "Mrs. Newcomb, the librarian, told us that," she said. "And she said it had a secret hiding place. Is that true?"

"Well . . . yes."

"May I see it?" asked Kit eagerly. She explained about the article she hoped to write for the newspaper.

"I'm afraid I cannot show it to you now," Miss Mundis answered, lowering her voice. "I don't want to frighten the time travelers away." She sank into a chair at the table. Her cat leaped into her lap.

Time travelers again! "Tell me about them," urged Kit.

"They came last week. I nearly telephoned the police when I first heard noises—bumps in the night, and footsteps on the stairs. Then I saw them with my own eyes, running through the garden! I only saw them from the back, but I could see they were wearing long dresses and old-timey bonnets like my grandmother used to wear. Later when I went down in the cellar to check that leaking pipe, I saw that the entrance to the secret room was open." Her voice was a whisper now. "The secret room must be a time portal! People from the past must be using it to come to the present day."

"Time portal?" Kit repeated, bewildered.

Miss Mundis raised her eyebrows. "Are you a skeptic like your great-uncle?"

"I don't know." Kit shrugged. "I just like things to make sense." She hesitated, watching Miss Mundis's smile broaden. "That's why I want to be a reporter when I grow up. Reporters deal with facts."

"Yes, of course," said the old woman, settling herself in her armchair and putting her feet up on the footstool. "But what are facts, really, except things we've already proven? There could be lots of other almost-facts out there, still waiting for proof. It's as William Shakespeare wrote in his play *Hamlet*: 'There are more things in heaven and earth, Horatio, than are dreamt of in your philosophy.' Prince Hamlet is saying there are things we can't even begin to dream of, because we don't have the concepts for them. But that doesn't mean they're not possible. We just don't see the big picture."

Kit frowned, thinking this over. "And the big picture has time portals in it? Like—time *doorways*?"

"Maybe so." Miss Mundis nodded approvingly. "Now tell me, have you ever heard of the writer H.G. Wells?"

Kit shook her head.

"You must read some of his books! My favorite is *The Time Machine*."

And as Kit cracked eggs into a skillet for Miss Mundis's supper, Miss Mundis talked about time travel. "Science fiction is based on possibilities of *science*," Miss Mundis explained eagerly. "We always think we know what's true and what's false, but people once believed that the sun revolved around the earth, and the earth was flat, and the stars in the sky were gods! Today, most people think time travel happens only in fiction. I think someday science will prove otherwise."

Kit flipped the eggs, thinking about stepping through a door into a time when buggies pulled by horses drove along the roads, with hoopskirted ladies riding inside. The back of her neck prickled. Was time travel possible? Or was Miss Mundis as batty as Uncle Hendrick believed?

Kit washed the frying pan and then glanced at the clock on the kitchen wall. "I'm forgetting I still need to help Uncle Hendrick! Will you be all right here on your own—I mean, can you get around on your bad foot?"

"The doctor came this morning and assured me rest will heal it," Miss Mundis said. "But he did say I should keep off my foot. So, my dear,

I'm wondering whether you might sleep here for a night this weekend. It would be helpful to have an able-bodied girl to look after me for a day or two."

Kit felt a tingle of excitement along her shoulder blades. "Yes, I'd like to! I'll ask my parents." She was eager to help Miss Mundis, but even more eager to find out more about Rivermead Manor and whatever it was that was happening there. *If there are such things as time travelers, I want to see them for myself,* she thought. *And I want to see that secret room!*

Kit walked next door to Uncle Hendrick's house, burning with curiosity about Rivermead and the family that had built it. "Did your parents know Miss Mundis's parents well?" she asked her uncle.

"Not at all. The Mundis family was too grand for the likes of us," said Uncle Hendrick. He frowned. "I was with Elsie at school, until her mother took her off to a fancy finishing school in Europe. The fool woman hoped her daughter would marry an English lord or some

such nonsense." He laughed, then broke off
abruptly. "So, how is she doing all by herself in
that grand manor? Foot all better now?"

As Kit dusted, she told her great-uncle about
Miss Mundis's twisted ankle, and the request
that Kit spend a night there this weekend. "I
can't fix the leaky pipe in the cellar, and I can't
replace the burned-out lightbulbs because Miss
Mundis doesn't have any new bulbs, but I can
do some more cleaning. I can also make sandwiches for Miss Mundis to keep in the icebox,
like I do here."

"And speaking of sandwiches . . ." said
Uncle Hendrick.

Kit went to the kitchen to make his supper.
As she worked, her great-uncle stood in the
doorway and grumbled at her for slicing the
meat too thickly, and for dropping crumbs when
she cut the bread.

You are a very grumpy old man! Kit thought
to herself, but she kept a pleasant expression on
her face as she wiped up the crumbs and hung
the dishrag neatly on the hook by the sink. She

set the platter of sandwiches on the table, then gathered up her schoolbag and jacket.

"Don't leave without your wages, girl," said Uncle Hendrick, handing her two dimes.

"Thank you." Then she blinked in surprise when, rather than seeing her out the door as he usually did, he took his hat and coat off the rack.

"I'll drive you home," he said.

"Why, thank you, Uncle Hendrick," said Kit, pleased by his unexpected offer.

They walked outside to the carriage house. Uncle Hendrick had told her that before the days of automobiles, it had sheltered both buggies and the horses that pulled them. Now Uncle Hendrick's automobile stood in solitary splendor in the shadowy building. He strode to the tool bench and snatched a rag from it. Kit waited while he wiped at some invisible spot on the automobile's hood and replaced the rag. "All right, hop in," he said.

When he dropped Kit off, Uncle Hendrick surprised Kit again by walking her to the door and staying while she asked permission to spend the weekend at Rivermead. "I can vouch that my neighbor is a respectable woman," he said to Kit's parents. "It would be charitable of you to allow Kit to help out."

Kit's father asked her mother, "Can you spare Kit from her chores here?"

Mrs. Kittredge smiled at Kit. "Now that Mrs. Howard is back on her feet again, we'll be fine. So if Kit wants to stay over, she may. What do you say, Kit?"

"I'd love to!"

Uncle Hendrick made a harrumphing sound. Then he said that he would pick Kit up the next day after lunch and drive her and her overnight bag to Rivermead Manor.

"Thank you," said Kit. *And then I'll see if there are more things in heaven and earth, as Hamlet said.*

5
A DINNERTIME INTERRUPTION

Mrs. Kittredge handed Kit the cheese grater. "We'll serve cheese on the side so that people can have their chili 'three-way' if they want it. But that's all the cheese we have left for the week, so go easy."

Kit grated the cheese into a bowl. Cincinnati's popular chili recipe called for it to be served "two-way"—chili sauce over noodles, or "three-way"—chili and noodles topped with cheese. Three-way was Kit's favorite.

A knock sounded at the back door just as she set the grater aside. Kit opened the door to find Ruthie breathless on the step.

"Hello, Ruthie," said Mrs. Kittredge. "We're just about to eat, dear."

"I don't mean to interrupt. My parents said

I could run over for a minute." Ruthie took a deep breath. "I just wanted to invite Kit and Stirling to my house tomorrow. My mother says we may search our attic to find props for our Underground Railroad project."

Once Ruthie would have just picked up her telephone, but ever since the Kittredges had canceled their phone service to save money, the only way to get in touch was to write a letter or stop by in person.

"I'm going to stay with Miss Mundis tomorrow," Kit told her friend, and she quickly explained about the plan to help on the weekend. "But I'm not leaving till after lunch, so I can still come over in the morning, can't I, Mother?"

Mrs. Kittredge nodded. "You may go after breakfast, as soon as your chores are done. Now why don't you ask if Stirling may join you." She directed Ruthie through the swinging door into the dining room, where the boarders were all gathered for their meal. Kit followed.

Everyone except Mr. West knew Ruthie, so Mrs. Kittredge introduced her. "This is Ruthie

Smithens. She's invited Stirling and Kit to work on a school project tomorrow morning."

"We're doing a play," Stirling added.

Mr. West looked at Ruthie. "Smithens, did you say? As in Mr. Smithens at the bank? *That* Smithens?"

Ruthie smiled tentatively. "Yes, sir. You know my father?"

"I'll say I do!" Mr. West's face darkened. "The scoundrel foreclosed on my house! Left me in the street!"

Ruthie flushed. Kit's mother placed her hand on Ruthie's shoulder as if to protect her from the man's anger. Kit's father stood up from his place at the head of the table. "The Smithenses are our friends, Mr. West. Mr. Smithens is a generous and honest man. I'll not have you sit at my table and insult him."

"I intended no insult," Mr. West said. "I apologize, young lady. But surely the banker's family lives in a nice large house. Is your father renting rooms to those who are less fortunate?"

A Dinnertime Interruption

Mrs. Kittredge put her arm around Ruthie and led her from the dining room into the front hallway. "Stirling and Kit will be over in the morning after their chores are done." She opened the front door. "Good night, Ruthie."

Kit followed Ruthie out into the cold air. "Sorry about Mr. West," Kit muttered. "That was so rude!"

Kit's family had almost lost their own home to the same bank, and she remembered the anguish her family had felt when their home was in danger. She felt a flicker of sympathy for Mr. West, but she understood that it was not Mr. Smithens's fault that Mr. West had lost his home. Hoping to cheer up her friend, she switched the subject. "I'm hoping to solve a mystery when I'm at Miss Mundis's house!" Kit told her.

Ruthie's sad expression faded. "That sounds exciting!"

Kit hurriedly told Ruthie what Miss Mundis had said about the time travelers in her house. "Of course Uncle Hendrick says all the science fiction stories she reads make her believe in things like time portals and rockets to the moon! He thinks she's losing her mind."

"Is that what you think, too?" asked Ruthie.

"She does say strange things . . . but I just don't know. Maybe I'll know more after tomorrow night."

"If it's not time travelers, then maybe it's *ghosts*," said Ruthie, hugging herself as if to ward off a sudden chill.

❧

"Times are hard," Mr. West was saying when Kit sat down and scooped the last of the cheese onto her chili. "How'd Smithens like it if *his* kid ended up in an orphanage because he couldn't keep a roof over her head?"

"Those orphanages!" Mr. Peck said. "Some kids run away rather than stay in one. I read in the paper that five kids took off from the Goodmont orphanage just last week."

"Terrible conditions everywhere," sighed

Mr. Bell. "The hobo camp grows more crowded every week."

Kit listened to this catalogue of misery, thinking about Jessamine's family. Where were they living? Was she homeless? She thought about how long the Depression had been going on. When would it end?

Time travelers would be pretty disappointed to come through a time portal and find themselves here and now, Kit thought—*unless they came from a time when folks were even worse off, like when people were trying to get to freedom on the Underground Railroad.*

Misery was relative, Kit decided.

6

SECRET IN THE ATTIC

On Saturday morning Kit served breakfast, then dusted the boarders' bedrooms while they were eating. She and Stirling did their math homework, and finally they were ready to go to Ruthie's. Mrs. Kittredge reminded Kit to be home by noon.

The houses on Ruthie's street were larger than Kit's, but not nearly as grand as those in Uncle Hendrick's neighborhood. Ruthie opened the door as they came up the walk. She rushed them into the kitchen to greet her parents, then bounced ahead of them up the stairs to the attic. She seemed full of energy and eager to get started on their hunt for props.

"We'll need some old-fashioned clothing," said Kit.

SECRET IN THE ATTIC

Ruthie's attic was larger than Kit's. One side was lined with neatly labeled boxes. The other side of the attic room contained a rocking chair, rolled-up rugs, and a baby's cradle that Kit thought must have been Ruthie's. Nothing seemed especially old.

"Let's check by the windows," Ruthie suggested. "There's an antique desk—and some suitcases . . ."

While Stirling opened the suitcases, Kit explored the drawers of the desk—all disappointingly empty—and Ruthie carefully ran her hand along the beams at the top of the wall to see if anything had been stored there. "Oh my goodness!" she cried out, pulling down a cobweb-covered little book. "Look at this!"

"What is it?" asked Stirling.

"It looks like an old diary!" Kit's heart leaped.

Ruthie dusted it off. "It *is* a diary!" she cried. "Oh, Kit—look! It says it's the diary of someone called Mary Jane."

Reverently, Kit took the book from Ruthie

and opened the yellowed pages carefully. She sucked in her breath. "Look—look at the date! 1852 . . ." Her voice trailed off.

She felt as if time had stopped. She hardly noticed that Ruthie and Stirling were there with her, wanting to see the book too. From somewhere downstairs she could hear voices— Ruthie's parents laughing—and she could smell coffee . . . but nothing seemed as real as the historical document in her hand. "This is amazing."

She squinted at the spidery handwriting. "October 10th, 1852," Kit read aloud, her voice trembling a little. These words had been hidden away for decades, written by a girl who had lived in this house long ago. *This is time travel, for real,* Kit marveled as she read:

"October 10th, 1852. Papa is bringing another cartload of hay up from the river. I know what that means! Under the hay will be people— escaping slaves from Kentucky. We must keep them safe."

Kit sucked in her breath. This was the sort of primary source that all reporters longed for. Words written by an eyewitness to history! This diary would be a wonderful help to her in writing her article for the newspaper: words right from the pen of someone who had been helping people escape on the Underground Railroad!

She turned the page. Stirling listened, wide-eyed. Ruthie pressed her hands to her mouth as Kit read:

"October 11th, 1852. I spent the day helping Mama make food for the travelers. I am helping to bake bread and cakes for them to take on their journey to freedom. They will leave in the morning."

"Just think!" said Kit. "Mary Jane might have been exactly our age. I wonder how long her family lived here. I wonder what became of her when she grew up!" Kit's eyes shone.

Kit ran her hand along the beams overhead

but found nothing else. She held the diary tightly. This was treasure enough.

"I think we should show the diary to your parents," Stirling said. "They'll know something about the family who used to live here."

"But it's almost noon," said Ruthie. "You two have to be going!"

"Is it that late?" asked Kit. "Oh, we do have to go, but I long to read this whole diary! May I borrow it, Ruthie? Mr. Gibbs at the newspaper says something like this is a reporter's gold!" Kit twirled around in excitement, clapping her hands.

Ruthie looked uncomfortable.

"Please, Ruthie," begged Kit. "I'll be very careful, and I'll bring it back tomorrow. I promise!"

"Well, all right," Ruthie agreed reluctantly.

Kit tucked the diary carefully into her skirt pocket as they went downstairs.

She heard Mrs. Smithens call to Ruthie from the kitchen, but Ruthie hurried them down the hallway and opened the front door. "See you later," she said.

Ruthie closed the door behind them. Kit kept her hand on the diary and bounced down the sidewalk with Stirling at her side. She couldn't wait to read the rest of the diary and start writing her article.

"It's only eleven o'clock," said Stirling as they headed around the corner toward home.

"What?" Pulled from her reverie, Kit glanced at him.

"I saw the clock on the wall in the Smithenses' hallway. Eleven o'clock. Not noon. We could have stayed a whole other hour at Ruthie's," he said.

"Oh—really?" Kit shrugged. She had the diary; nothing was more interesting than that.

"We didn't have to leave so early," Stirling repeated quietly. "I wonder why Ruthie wanted us gone?"

7

STIRLING SMELLS A RAT

"Well, now we have more time to read Mary Jane's diary." Kit took the book out of her pocket as they walked along. She was surprised Stirling didn't seem more excited. But there was no telling what would interest boys.

"Listen to this, Stirling! *October 12th, 1852. We got up before dawn and helped the slaves into the wagon. Mama gave them blankets and pillows and the food we made. I gave the little girl my favorite doll to take with her. Then we piled the hay back on top of them all, and the horses set off . . .*

"Isn't it strange to think of all this happening right in Ruthie's house?" Kit said. "I didn't know her house was even that old! Well, maybe it's just their furnishings that make it seem so modern. Her parents like things in the latest styles . . ."

STIRLING SMELLS A RAT

Kit turned the page. "Listen to this: *November 20th, 1852. Mama and I have been making more bread, so we shall be ready when the poor, tired slaves arrive. Papa tells us another shipment of 'hay' is on its way, this time from West Virginia . . .*"

She tried to turn the page, but two pages were stuck together. She stopped to ease them apart.

"Careful," said Stirling.

Kit didn't tear the pages. But when she separated the yellowed pages, she was surprised to see that the page in between had a small area of clean white paper, a jagged island of white surrounded by faded yellow. "This is odd . . ." she said.

"Here, let me see." Stirling reached for the little book. He ran his fingers over the white area, then frowned. He turned to the next entry, lifted the diary to his nose, and sniffed deeply. "Kit, I smell a rat."

Kit had to grin. "A *rat*? Well, I smell *coffee*! Isn't that odd? I smelled it at Ruthie's house, and now I smell it here, too."

"Something isn't right," Stirling said. "It's this diary that smells of coffee! And the white part on this page doesn't look old at all."

Kit grabbed the book and paged through it. He was right—the white area didn't look old. She could hear her heartbeat thudding in her head as she flipped open the diary to the last entry she'd read aloud. "Stirling—look here. This entry says the slaves are coming from West Virginia."

"I know," he said.

She stared at him. "But Mr. Leiser was just teaching us about how West Virginia split off from Virginia *during* the Civil War. Not *before* it! There was no *West* Virginia in 1852." She felt disappointment tingling inside her. "The book must be a fake. Oh, crumbs! Wait till Ruthie hears."

Something about Stirling's expression stopped her. "What?" she demanded.

Stirling just shrugged.

And then Kit understood. "You think Ruthie already knows?"

"The book smells like coffee, Kit," he said quietly.

"You mean . . . you think Ruthie stained the pages with coffee to make them look old?"

He nodded.

Kit felt like crying. "She soaked them, and then dried them . . . that's why they're so warped! And the cobwebs—?"

"She could have found cobwebs and draped them over the book." Stirling raised his eyebrows. "It's pretty clever. But the way she hurried us out of the house so that we couldn't show the book to her parents was strange. And when you said you didn't think Ruthie's house was old enough to have been on the Underground Railroad, I started thinking."

"*West* Virginia . . ." Kit's voice turned bitter. "I guess Ruthie wasn't listening in class." She felt hot with disappointment, and sick with anger and embarrassment. Why would her best friend play a trick on her?

❦

Kit held her fury inside as she sat with her parents and her uncle at the dining room table eating vegetable soup and triangles of toast. Her parents chatted with Uncle Hendrick, but Kit remained silent. She felt she would choke on her food if she tried to tell them about the diary.

But once her overnight case was packed and she had kissed her parents good-bye, Kit climbed into Uncle Hendrick's automobile and asked if he would stop at Ruthie's house. "I need to return something," Kit said.

"Make it snappy," he said. "We want to get to Rivermead before Elsie flies off with the little green men."

Kit jumped out of the motorcar. She rang Ruthie's bell.

"Why, hello, Kit," said Mrs. Smithens, opening the door. She saw the automobile at the curb. "Would you and your uncle like to come in?"

"No thanks," Kit said. "I have something for Ruthie."

"She's in the kitchen. Go on in."

Kit found Ruthie at the table eating creamed

chicken. She thrust the diary at Ruthie. "It's a fake!" she said, tears of hurt and fury welling in her eyes. "Why would you do such a thing?"

"You said you longed to find an old diary," Ruthie whispered. "I-I was just trying to make that happen for you."

"You just don't get it. I'd absolutely *love* to find an old diary—of course I would! But not a fake one! Can't you see that's no fun at all?" Kit couldn't even tell Ruthie how sick with disappointment she felt, and how humiliated she was at having acted so excited in front of her and Stirling. Twirling around! How foolish she must have looked. How *gullible*.

She turned away, not even looking back when Ruthie called her name.

Kit ran out of the house and jumped onto the running board of Uncle Hendrick's big automobile waiting at the curb. She climbed in and settled herself next to him on the leather seat. "I'll never speak to Ruthie again," she muttered as they drove away.

8

FOOTPRINTS IN THE DUST

Kit stared out the window while Uncle Hendrick drove across town. She was relieved that Uncle Hendrick didn't pepper her with questions the way he usually did. It suited her to sit quietly. In her head she was remembering the excitement of finding the diary—and the crushing disappointment of realizing it was a hoax. In her mind's eye she pictured herself, over and over, twirling around in Ruthie's attic. Kit's cheeks flamed despite the cold air in the car. Uncle Hendrick glanced over at her.

"Feeling poorly?" he asked. "It won't do to show up at Elsie's with a fever. You're there to look after her—not the other way around."

"I'm fine," said Kit stoutly, and resolved not to think about Ruthie's treachery.

Uncle Hendrick pulled up to the curb in front of Rivermead. Kit thanked him and reached for her suitcase, but Uncle Hendrick was already lifting it out and striding with it through the gate. Kit scurried behind him.

Miss Mundis opened the door at his knock. She leaned heavily on a cane. "So good to see you, dear girl," she said to Kit. Then she nodded at Uncle Hendrick. "Hello, Hen," she added. "How have you been?"

"Never better," he said gruffly.

"Would you like to come in?" She stood aside, opening the door wider.

Uncle Hendrick shook his head. "Just don't let your little green men carry Kit off, all right?" He chuckled at his own wit. "Send her over tomorrow when you're tired of her, and I'll see that she gets home."

Miss Mundis watched him stride away. Then she closed the door and locked it.

"I've already had two visitors today, and the hallway between the kitchen and the front door seems to get longer each time." She sighed, taking Kit's arm for support. "But you're here now. Come make us a pot of tea."

"Who came to see you?" asked Kit as they walked to the kitchen.

"A hobo wanting to rake the yard, and your Mr. West." Miss Mundis picked Stanley up out of the chair and smoothed his fur. "And you didn't like him one bit, did you, boy?" She cuddled the cat.

Stanley let out a loud *meow*.

Kit had to laugh. "Please don't call him *my* Mr. West. I think he's a very strange person. But why didn't Stanley like him?"

"Because he was after me again to open a boarding house, that's why! And Stanley doesn't take to pushy strangers." She stroked his head, but her eyes were on Kit. "Maybe you can tell him that for me, Kit, when you see him at your house. Tell him enough is enough, and I won't be bullied—or charmed—into anything I don't want to do."

"I will tell him," said Kit. "But what do you mean, charmed? I haven't seen him be charming at all. But I have seen him be a bully." She remembered how he'd insulted Ruthie's father, and felt her face flush with anger. Then she reminded herself that she didn't care about Ruthie anymore.

Miss Mundis set the cat down and started shuffling through the stack of magazines next to her chair. "Now, don't tell me the man is a thief as well as a nuisance!"

"Something's missing?"

"It was here," Miss Mundis told Kit. "My brand-new issue of *Amazing Stories*. I'd marked a time travel story for you. I was reading it when I got up to answer the doorbell. I carried the magazine with me. Mr. West told me he also reads it. We started talking about our favorite stories, and I almost forgot that I didn't like him." She chuckled. "But where is it?"

Miss Mundis settled into her chair with her cat on her lap and watched as Kit made and served the tea.

"You know, Mr. West's idea about the board-ing house isn't really a bad one," Miss Mundis said musingly. One gnarled hand held her tea-cup, and the other hand stroked Stanley, draped across her lap. "If I were younger, we might quite like running a boarding house, mightn't we, Stanley? If only you could be some help!" She smiled at Kit. "Of course I can't do a thing now, not with my bad ankle and my aching joints. And as long as the time travelers keep coming through, I don't want to disturb them. As long as they need to use the time portal, I will keep the house just as it is. Except for repairs, of course. I'd like to fix things up a bit."

Kit wanted to quiz Miss Mundis about the time travelers, but she knew she should get to work. "What can I do now?" she asked.

"Bless your heart. Well, I'd ask you to start by changing the lightbulb that's burned out in the upstairs bathroom above the mirror, but I still have no new bulbs. So why don't you mop up the water on the cellar floor? Stanley and I will listen to the radio in the parlor."

Kit gathered some old rags and the mop in the pantry and carried them down the cellar steps. But at the bottom of the steps she stopped, confused. There was no trace of water from the broken pipe.

Maybe the leak was in the laundry room, she thought. Quickly she crossed the stone floor of the main room, peeking into the laundry with its tub and washboard. The floor was dry, and there was no sign of a leaking pipe. She looked into the storage room, with shelves holding jars of jam and summer pickles, and a room full of old tools that had probably belonged to Miss Mundis's father long ago. There was a workbench with some clay flowerpots stacked on it, jars of screws and nails, and a basket lined with a soft white towel. It was full of lightbulbs— a dozen of them, packed neatly. Kit frowned. Miss Mundis had said she was out of lightbulbs.

She must have forgotten these, thought Kit. She lingered, looking around her.

Where was the secret room?

Of course, it wouldn't be a very good secret room if you could discover it just by walking past, Kit thought wryly.

Carrying the basket of lightbulbs, Kit went back up the cellar stairs and down the hall to the parlor.

"Done so soon?" Miss Mundis beamed at Kit. "My, you're a quick helper!"

Kit set the basket of bulbs on the low table by the sofa. "The cellar was dry," Kit admitted. "And you do have lightbulbs. I found this basket in the cellar and brought them up so you'll have them if you need them."

A look of astonishment crossed Miss Mundis's face. "But . . . why—I don't know how . . ." she began. Then the confusion left her eyes. "Those lovely time travelers! They're looking after me. It's their way of saying thank you."

Kit looked at Miss Mundis quizzically. Did the old lady really believe time travelers had mopped her cellar and purchased lightbulbs? But before Kit could ask, Miss Mundis was instructing her on her next task.

"Now you can take your overnight case upstairs to the room next to mine—the blue bedroom. Take a bulb with you. You can replace the lightbulb in the bathroom while you're up there."

Kit chose a bulb from the basket, then grabbed her case, which she'd left by the front door, and crossed the hall to the curving staircase. She stopped to admire the carved newel post. How smooth the wooden banister was! It would be fun to sit at the top and slide down all the way to the bottom . . .

"Go ahead," called a quavery voice from the parlor, and Kit looked through the double doors to where Miss Mundis sat on a high-backed sofa with her cat at her side and a smile on her face. "I used to slide down that banister when I was a girl your age."

"You read my mind!" Kit cried.

"Not hard to do when I see a young girl standing at the bottom of that staircase," replied Miss Mundis with a laugh.

Kit climbed the stairs. The top step creaked dramatically. She stopped, blinking in surprise at the long, elegant hallway before her, lined with closed doors. There must be, what—six, seven, *eight* bedrooms?

She walked down the hallway, opening doors
and peering inside. The furniture was draped
with white sheets, creating a ghostly look. Kit
closed the doors softly and continued down the
hall till she found a bedroom with an open door.
She peeked inside. *This is where Miss Mundis
sleeps,* she thought.

There was a four-poster bed covered in a
faded red and yellow quilt, with a stack of science fiction magazines on the bedside table.
Kit leaned over to see the photos on the dresser
more clearly. Kit recognized a much younger
Miss Mundis—with the same wide smile—wearing an old-fashioned bathing costume with long
black stockings, a knee-length skirt, and flat black
shoes that laced up her legs. *I'd sink if I had to swim
in that,* Kit thought. Next to her stood a young
man who looked very much like Kit's brother,
Charlie—except that Charlie wouldn't be caught
dead wearing such a silly striped bathing suit.

A loud *meow* from the doorway startled Kit,
and she turned guiltily to find Stanley the cat
staring at her.

"You're right," she said. "I'm being nosy, aren't I?"

The next room was hers. *The blue bedroom,* thought Kit, and the name fit perfectly. A large four-poster bed was covered in a soft blue woolen blanket, and a folded quilt waited at the end of the bed, patterned in cornflowers that matched the wallpaper. Kit set down her luggage and the lightbulb. She opened her suitcase and took out her nightgown and robe. Then she grabbed the lightbulb and went in search of the burned-out light.

The bathroom next door, tiled in white, had a high, old-fashioned toilet and a porcelain bathtub with silver clawed feet. She flipped the light switch to see which bulb was burned out. Then she found a step stool in the corner and climbed up on it to change the bulb. She flipped the switch a few times just to ensure that the light was working. *On. Off.* As she watched light flood the room, a funny thought struck her. How would time travelers from the past know to buy lightbulbs? They probably didn't even have electric lights back then.

There was no sense discussing this with Miss Mundis, Kit knew. The elderly woman seemed convinced that time travelers were using her home, and she accepted their gifts and services as payment for their safe passage through the time portal. Kit hated to admit it, but she was beginning to agree with Uncle Hendrick that Miss Mundis was a little bit batty!

Kit walked back down the hallway to the top of the stairs and then threw one leg over the banister as if she were mounting a horse. She pushed off with her hands—*wheeeee!*—and slid all the way down to the post at the foot of the stairs. She imagined Miss Mundis doing the same thing when she was Kit's age.

❧

After supper Miss Mundis instructed Kit to light a fire in the parlor fireplace. Soon a cheer-ful blaze was warming the room. Miss Mundis patted the sofa. "I like to read in the evening. Feel free to join me."

But there was something Kit wanted to do first. "We're performing a skit at school," she told Miss Mundis. "I'm wondering if I could look up in your attic for props." She pushed down the memory of searching for props up in Ruthie's attic that morning. Thinking of the hoax made her feel like crying.

"You won't find much, my dear. I went through generations of junk a couple of years ago. Tossed the worst and sold the best. A place the size of Rivermead takes money to keep up, you know. The property used to be nearly double the size, but my great-grandfather sold off land to pay taxes. Your uncle's house was built on what used to be our land. Our house's original carriage house is now on his property! Anyway, feel free to look in the attic. Take a broom up with you, please. The floor will surely need sweeping."

At the top of the long flight of stairs was a door with a cold porcelain knob. The door swung open into darkness. Kit reached along the wall to press the button for the light. A single bulb dangling from a wire lit the large, bare room. Kit breathed out in a huff of disappointment. Just as Miss Mundis had said, the attic had been cleaned out. There were no props for their project.

The ceilings were higher than those in Ruthie's house. Kit would not be able to run her hand along the beams in search of a real hidden diary.

Sighing in disappointment, Kit started sweeping the floor. Then she stopped.

There in the dust were footprints.

Small barefoot prints, and larger prints, too. Some of the prints were smudged; some were more clearly defined. A piece of fabric lay crumpled on the floor. Kit picked it up and stared. It was a faded bonnet—the sort girls had worn a hundred years ago.

9
THE HIDDEN ROOM

Kit hurried down the narrow staircase, carrying the bonnet. She needed to tell Miss Mundis that someone had been in her attic and—Kit stopped at the top of the curving stairs leading down to the front hallway. *And what?* she thought. *Slow down.*

Maybe she was just getting spooked by the big old house, by the repairs that had been done mysteriously, and by Miss Mundis's talk of time travelers.

Kit ran her hand over the smooth wood of the banister. Did she really believe that time travelers had mopped up water in the cellar and bought lightbulbs to thank Miss Mundis for the use of her secret room? Did she really believe that time travelers had left their footprints and this bonnet in the attic?

Or was something else going on?

Miss Mundis was reading by the fire. Kit dangled the bonnet by its long ties. "I found this in the attic," she said.

Miss Mundis frowned. "Why, I've never seen this before." A smile spread across her face. "Oh, Kit," she breathed. "This is the proof I've hoped for."

"There are also footprints," Kit told her. "Big and small. I didn't sweep them away."

Miss Mundis's eyes sparkled. "This I must see," she said, using her cane to stand. Then she winced and sank back down. "When my ankle is stronger, that is. Now it's my bedtime."

After she had climbed the stairs to her bedroom, Miss Mundis's ankle was painful and swollen. Kit helped her to bed, treated the injured ankle with a cold-water compress, and then wrapped it in a clean cloth bandage.

Miss Mundis thanked her. "That feels better already." She switched off her bedside lamp. "Good night, Kit," she said. "Sweet dreams. And remember: 'There are more things in heaven and earth, Horatio, than are dreamt of in your philosophy.'"

Kit furrowed her brow. "Like—we see only the tip of the iceberg?"

"Exactly!" Miss Mundis handed Kit several magazines from her bedside table. "A little something to sweeten your dreams," she said. "Sleep tight!"

Soon Kit lay in bed, but she felt wide-awake. Bemused, she reached for the first magazine. She was quickly caught up in the fantastical stories.

In *Astounding Stories of Super-Science* she read "The Atom-Smasher," where an evil professor made a time machine that shot him all the way back to the time of dinosaurs. In *Amazing Stories* she read "The Man Who Saw the Future," about Henri, a man from France in the year 1444, who traveled five hundred years forward to 1944 and then home again. When he tried to describe the things he'd seen—machines flying through the sky and voices coming out of a box and carriages moving along without horses to pull them—people thought he was a sorcerer!

The strange stories made Kit think of all the other things people had once thought were impossible. Flying machines? When Miss Mundis was young, there were no airplanes at all. And now they had Amelia Earhart winging her way across the ocean. Mr. Leiser talked about inventions that had changed the world. What would the early settlers in America have thought about lights coming on with the flip of a switch, or a machine that allowed you to talk to people miles away? And yet electric lights and telephones were common now.

So what was fact and what was fiction?

The mattress was soft, with a deep groove in the center that cradled her. Kit wondered about all the children who might have slept in this bed over the hundred years since Rivermead Manor had been built. What if she traveled back through a time portal and met Miss Mundis right here—as a girl her own age? Would old Miss Mundis recognize Kit when she returned to her present time? For the first time, Kit began to see the appeal of fantasy. She knew Ruthie would love to read the stories in these magazines.

Again, a stab of sadness pricked Kit at the thought of Ruthie.

Then, eyes wide open in the unfamiliar darkness, Kit heard something overhead, and all thoughts of Ruthie vanished. It came again—a soft noise—a shuffle.

Mice?

Or the soft pad of bare feet?

Kit slid out of bed, shivering in the cold room. She pulled on her robe and hugged herself for warmth, listening hard. From the open door of the bedroom next to hers came the sound of a faint snore. Rain pattered against the windows.

Was there an intruder in the house? If so, they must call the police. She was glad that Miss Mundis's telephone was working, unlike the one on the wall in Kit's own house.

She slid her feet into her slippers and crept to

the door. She sucked in her breath as something white flashed past in the hallway—the flick of a long skirt? Or was it just Stanley, prowling the house? There was a shuffling sound at the stairs. Kit edged out into the hallway and peered down the stairs to the shadowy entrance hall. No cat.

Pale moonlight filtered through the stained glass over the door. Nobody was in the hall.

Kit exhaled slowly and slipped down the stairs. Was that whispering she heard faintly coming from the kitchen—or just rain against the windows?

She padded into the kitchen and froze.

Between the wide wooden boards of the kitchen floor, through the same crack that the penny had fallen into, Kit saw a sliver of light. It seemed otherworldly—as if there were time travelers, lanterns held high, emerging from the long-ago past into present-day Cincinnati.

Was someone in the cellar? She strained to listen. There was something that could have been the faintest whisper of voices and a quickly stifled giggle. The giggle of a child.

Or it could have been the furnace, or the old house settling.

Kit took a flashlight from the pantry shelf, then opened the door to the cellar, and tiptoed down the steps. She heard only the thick hush of silence. Could she have imagined it all?

But there it was again—a noise in the next room that sounded like the murmur of voices.

Kit held her breath, edging forward, shining her flashlight into the laundry room and across its walls. Her light illuminated the washtubs, the mangle, the ironing board, and—nothing else.

No one was there. But when she turned her flashlight toward the door to leave, it looked for just an instant as though a sliver of light remained behind, just visible between the boards that covered the far wall. How could that be?

The secret room?! Kit dropped to her knees and ran her hands over the boards.

She pressed at the top and bottom, and then

her fingers found a knothole. She stuck her finger into the knothole, and with a small scraping noise, a panel of wood slid back to reveal a small doorway, about three feet tall. Kit shone her light into a low-ceilinged space about eight feet square. It was no bigger than their linen closet at home.

It was dark now. And it was empty. Empty—except for something red in the corner. What had made the light she'd seen—if she'd even really seen it at all?

Taking a deep breath, Kit edged into the room. Would she be zapped into the past—or the future?

I don't believe in time travel, she told herself firmly.

The top of Kit's head nearly brushed the ceiling. She crossed the space in two large steps and snatched up the red thing—a ribbon. And wait—there was something else in the shadow. A slip of paper, raggedly torn.

Kit picked it up, backing out of the room. She closed the panel carefully, juggling the flashlight and the paper and the ribbon. Then she turned and ran back up the cellar stairs, the hairs on the back of her neck prickling.

Keeping the flashlight with her, she pelted through the kitchen and up the main stairs to her bedroom. She slid into bed and drew the soft blue bedspread up to her chin. Her heartbeat pounded in her head.

She slipped the ribbon under her pillow. Then she smoothed out the slip of paper. It was yellowed around the edges. Letters in faded black ink, in an angular hand, spelled out a message that made no sense:

> *and you have to realize*
> *how very desperate*
> *I have become—*

Had the message been written by desperate slaves long ago as they hid in the secret room, hoping to reach freedom? Was the note a hoax, like the fake diary?

She sniffed: no smell of coffee.

Kit tucked the paper under her pillow along-side the ribbon. Thoughts whirled as she lay with eyes wide open in the shadowy room. It was a long time before she finally fell asleep.

10
A LIST OF SUSPECTS

"Rise and shine!" Miss Mundis called, limping over to open the curtains. Kit stirred in her bed and blinked at the sun streaming in through the long windows.

"Good morning," she mumbled sleepily.

"Come down and we'll make waffles," said Miss Mundis.

"I love waffles," Kit said. "I'll make them while you rest your foot." She reached for her bathrobe, and slid the red ribbon and the note from under her pillow into the pocket.

"This will be a treat," Miss Mundis said. "I rarely get out the waffle iron for just me alone."

Downstairs at the kitchen door, Miss Mundis stopped with a gasp. Kit nearly ran into her. "What is it?" Kit asked.

"Purple asters," whispered Miss Mundis, pointing to the table where the morning sun glinted on a bouquet of flowers in a mason jar. "My favorite! How kind of you to bring them to me."

"But . . . I didn't," said Kit. "It wasn't me."

"No?" Miss Mundis chuckled. "Well, yesterday it was repairs around the house. Today it's flowers! Those time travelers are certainly kindly people."

Miss Mundis went to the icebox to get the ingredients for the waffles.

"That's odd," she said. "I was sure I had two bottles of milk in here. And now one's gone." She scratched her head in puzzlement. Then she brightened. "Of course! The asters must be their way of making up for the milk they took!"

Flowers, and now missing milk. Frowning, Kit checked the back door. It was locked. She darted down the long hall to the front door and found it also locked securely. No one had entered that way in the night.

Kit had enjoyed the time travel stories in the

magazines, but she couldn't stretch her mind enough to believe that time travelers were doing chores and drinking milk and bringing gifts.

Something very strange was going on at Rivermead Manor.

Her hand slipped into her bathrobe pocket and fingered the little piece of paper. Was it connected to what was happening in this house?

Because something *was* happening. And if not visits from time travelers, then what?

Had Miss Mundis found some asters in the tangled garden and picked them—and then forgotten? Or had she put them on the table deliberately to baffle Kit, and was she only *pretending* to believe that time travelers had brought them? But when would she have had a chance to pick flowers anyway, with her injured foot? Kit had been with her nearly every moment yesterday afternoon and evening.

Feeling unsettled, Kit made the waffles. Miss Mundis ate with gusto. Kit brought her own plate to the table and sat across from the elderly lady. She followed Miss Mundis's example and drenched one waffle with maple syrup and spread the other with strawberry preserves. Syrup was a luxury Kit didn't get at home anymore. As she ate, Kit observed Miss Mundis from beneath her lashes.

A loud knocking on the front door startled them. Stanley streaked under the armchair. "Oh dear," said Miss Mundis. "What now?"

"I'll take care of it," Kit assured her. She went to the front door. Immediately the visitor thrust a small box into her hands.

"Mr. West!" She looked down at the box. "You've brought chocolates?"

Their lodger seemed even more surprised to see Kit than she was to see him. "Why. . . Kit Kittredge! What are you doing in this neighborhood?"

"I work for Miss Mundis," she replied. "Can I help you?"

He frowned down at her and cleared his throat. "Ahem . . . The chocolates, of course, are for your employer. *Not* for little girls!"

Kit flushed. "She's busy now, but I'll

give them to her. Thank you." She hesitated. "Did you take her magazine when you left yesterday?"

"Of course not!"

She started to close the door, but he put his hand out and held it open.

"Just a minute. I've come to see about a very *important* matter of business."

"You've come to talk Miss Mundis into turning Rivermead Manor into a boarding house like ours," Kid said pertly. She wanted to protect Miss Mundis. "But she can't handle that."

As she started to close the door again, he reached out and caught her wrist. "Tell her I'm speaking for a lot of desperate men and women, Kit Kittredge," he said. "Times are hard, and desperate times require desperate measures."

Kit pulled her wrist out of his grip.

"I'm sorry," said Mr. West, though he didn't look sorry to Kit. "The old lady will come around, one way or another. Her heart's in the right place. Tell her I'll be back." Then he smiled at Kit. "I hope she likes the chocolates. Or does she prefer flowers?"

"Did *you* bring the asters?" she demanded. *But the doors were locked this morning,* she remembered.

"I don't know what you're talking about." He tipped his hat and turned away.

Unsettled, Kit closed the door and went back to the kitchen. She handed Miss Mundis the box of chocolates, and the old woman's face lit up.

"Flowers *and* chocolates!" Miss Mundis exclaimed. "This is shaping up to be a good morning, isn't it?"

"Well," said Kit, "something very odd is going on, and Mr. West may be part of it."

"Mr. West?" Miss Mundis looked intrigued.

Kit's brow furrowed. "It was Mr. West at the door. He said these are desperate times, and desperate times need desperate measures. I thought maybe *he* left the asters, but there's no sign that he broke into the house . . ."

"No, the time travelers left them," said Miss Mundis calmly. "I'm quite certain."

"But there's more." Kit related how she'd heard noises in the night and thought she'd seen a light in the cellar and found the secret room. She fished in her bathrobe pocket and brought out the red ribbon. "I found this."

Miss Mundis took it reverently. "Kit," she said, "I've been thinking. The bonnet you found and the clothes I saw the time travelers wearing were all from the days of slavery. What if the time travelers are escaping slavery through Rivermead Manor? What if this ribbon fell from a little girl's pigtails as she ran to freedom? Think of it, Kit!" In her excitement, she let the ribbon drop, and Stanley the cat pounced on it. Miss Mundis laughed in surprise.

Frustrated, Kit watched Stanley bat at the ribbon. It was no use trying to discuss the ribbon—or the scrap of paper—with Miss Mundis. Now she seemed more determined than ever to believe that time travelers were using her secret room to escape from their own time into *now*.

Kit decided to leave the folded paper scrap in her pocket. She did not want it to end up as a toy for Stanley. She felt sure it was a clue— to *something*.

❧

Miss Mundis settled into her armchair with her cat and a magazine. After changing into her clothes and making her bed, Kit dusted all the downstairs rooms. She gathered throw rugs and shook them out the back door. As she looked out into Miss Mundis's rain-spangled garden, her eye was caught by the sight of someone—a child— running through the trees. Kit squinted and stared harder. It was a girl—a girl with dark skin and dark hair in two braids.

Kit dashed outside, but the girl was gone. The big wooden swing hanging from a tall buckeye tree—a swing easily large enough to hold two adults—was swaying. Kit stared at it, as the memory of the tire swing behind the car lot flashed through her mind. Jessamine wore her hair in two braids. Kit thought back to their conversation that day at the library. Jessamine had said that her school was in the same direction, more or less, as Uncle Hendrick's house. Could Jessamine be here? But why would she be swinging in Miss Mundis's garden on a Sunday morning?

Slowly Kit walked across the lawn to perch on the swing. The morning was cool and the breeze was brisk, and Kit pumped high, recalling how she and Jessamine had swung together, spinning dizzily, shrieking with joy. She and Ruthie swung together on the school playground at recess, too, sharing secrets, singing songs, making plans. *I've missed Jessamine,* she thought. And then, with a sharp stab of loss: *And I miss Ruthie.*

❧

"How is Elsie?" Uncle Hendrick asked when Kit arrived. "Been abducted yet by the little green men?"

He asked Kit to make a sandwich for his lunch while he fussed with his automobile out in the carriage house.

She made a thick ham and cheese sandwich, thinking wistfully of how much food was stored in Uncle Hendrick's icebox—all for him!—and comparing it to the slim pickings in their own icebox at home. Mother had a genius for stretching a small amount of food to feed all their many boarders, but it was still very satisfying for Kit to cut the ham and the cheese in thick slices and lay them on the bread with mayonnaise and mustard. She made a sandwich for herself, too, and ate it standing at the counter.

She left her uncle's sandwich on the table, covered with a clean cloth, and went to find him in the carriage house.

Uncle Hendrick was washing the running boards of his motorcar. "Lunch is ready," Kit told him.

"Almost done," he said. "I like a clean car." She waited while he scrubbed and polished, trying to imagine the old-fashioned carriages that had once been kept here. After a few minutes, he dried the running boards with an old towel and emptied the bucket of water outside on the drive. They walked back to the house together.

In the kitchen Uncle Hendrick frowned in irritation. "So, where is my lunch?"

"Right there!" Kit pointed—then gasped. Although the plate still lay on the kitchen table where she'd left it, the sandwich and the cloth that had covered it were gone.

"I left your sandwich on that plate!" she insisted. "You know, Miss Mundis was missing a bottle of milk this morning. She thinks time travelers took it."

"Time travelers took her milk? Then I guess Martians took my sandwich." His voice deepened to a growl. "Never mind. Get your bag, and I'll take you home."

"Truly, Uncle Hendrick, I really did make you a ham and cheese sandwich! And I can make you another one—"

"Never mind that now. More likely a thieving hobo slipped into the house while we were outside."

Silently Kit followed her great-uncle out to the automobile. *Is that what happened to the sandwich? Taken—right under our noses!* Kit's thoughts were in turmoil. *By a hobo? Or does Uncle Hendrick have time travelers, too?*

Whoever had taken the sandwich must have been hungry, Kit reasoned. As they drove past Rivermead, she remembered the girl in the garden earlier. Could *Jessamine* have come to Uncle Hendrick's house and slipped into his kitchen while Kit was in the carriage house? Did Jessamine's family not have enough to eat?

11

LITTLE ORPHAN ANNIE

It felt strange walking to school without Ruthie on Monday. Kit worked hard and did not turn around in her seat to chat. At recess she remained inside to memorize her spelling words. She stayed out of Ruthie's way all day long. And as soon as Mr. Leiser dismissed the class, Kit grabbed her book bag and ran. She would go straight home. On Mondays she didn't work at Rivermead or for Uncle Hendrick.

As she was passing the road that led to Uncle Hendrick's neighborhood, Kit saw a figure walking up ahead, bent low with the effort of carrying a large canvas bag. Something about the girl's jacket looked familiar.

"Jessamine!" Kit shouted, but the other girl did not turn her head. "Hello there!" called Kit, certain that it was Jessamine. But Jessamine didn't seem to hear her.

Kit hurried after her, hoping to catch up. Jessamine kept her head down, almost running now.

The day was cold. Kit wrapped her red woolen scarf around her nose and mouth and was glad for her warm coat, even though it was getting small for her and pulled tightly across the shoulders. Jessamine, up ahead, must be even colder in her thin jacket, Kit thought.

Kit had to run to keep up, though Jessamine was burdened by her school satchel and the large canvas bag. She was *fast*. Kit remembered how they used to race each other from one end of the car lot behind the sales office to the other end. Jessamine had usually won.

Now they were heading in the direction of the river. Kit knew that the hobo camp was along the river, just beyond the railroad tracks. Is that where Jessamine was heading? Things were very bad indeed for Jessamine's family if they were living there.

Up ahead, Jessamine turned the corner—away from the river and toward the bottom of a gently sloping hill. The wind was blowing colder, and Kit knew that Mother would be expecting her home. But Jessamine kept walking, and Kit kept following. Another corner, and Jessamine was gone.

This was an unfamiliar part of town. Kit told herself she would climb to the top of the hill and go no farther. If she still hadn't caught sight of Jessamine, she'd head for home.

On the hilltop she found herself standing outside a large, ornate building. It looked even larger and shabbier than Rivermead Manor. The sign on the ornate entrance gate read *Goodmont Children's Home.*

Kit had heard about the children's home but had never seen it. She knew that orphans lived there, and Mrs. Smithens, Ruthie's mother, knew a couple who had adopted a baby from the home. And lately, since times had been so hard, she'd heard talk about "half orphans" living there—children whose parents had lost their homes and gone looking for work, like that lady hobo, Mrs. Addison.

Inside the tall fence, Kit could see children playing hopscotch in a windswept yard. Although the day was cold, they were barefoot. Kit saw a figure walking along the outside of the fence, beckoning to the girls.

Was that Jessamine? No, as Kit moved closer she could see that it was a woman—a white woman. It looked like the lady hobo, Mrs. Addison! Was she here to visit her children? Or maybe she was asking for work at the orphanage.

The girls stopped their game and came to the fence. The woman spoke to them, but Kit couldn't hear a word. Then the woman trudged away, and the girls ran back across the yard to confer with a small crowd of children kicking a ball.

Kit looked around for Jessamine. Her heart leaped when she spotted Jessamine darting around the side of the building, glancing back over her shoulder as if to check whether Kit was still following.

Oh, poor Jess. No wonder Jessamine had been hurrying away from Kit. She must be ashamed for anyone to know that she was living in an orphanage.

A fence bordered the back of the orphanage yard. As Jessamine moved carefully along the outside of it, Kit started after her and quickly caught up. "Jess!"

Jessamine spun around, wide-eyed. She put her finger to her lips. "Shh!"

"What's wrong?"

Jessamine ran to her, her dark eyes clouded. "Please be quiet, Kit. What do you want here? Why are you following me?"

"Well, I just wanted to talk to you! I see where you're living now, and . . ."

I wonder if Mother would let Jessamine live with us.

"Mind your own business," said Jessamine.

Speechless and hurt, Kit just stared at her. "Don't you want to be friends anymore?" she asked in a small voice.

Jessamine sighed. "Look, I have something

to do here, and it's . . . secret." She grabbed Kit's arm and pulled her over to a stand of golden buckeye trees. "Don't let anybody see us," she hissed in Kit's ear. "Keep well away from the fence."

Jessamine led Kit to a fallen log where two thin children sat. The girl wore a threadbare cotton dress and a patched cardigan. She looked to be about the same age as Kit and Jessamine. The boy was younger—maybe seven or eight. Both had dark curly hair and brown skin.

Who, wondered Kit, were these children? Were they orphans? Why were they sitting in the woods?

The boy jumped to his feet. "We thought you weren't coming!"

"I'm here now," said Jessamine, seating herself between them on the log.

"Who's *she*? the boy asked. The girl also peered at Kit, frowning.

"This is Kit," said Jessamine resignedly. "She wants to join us. Kit, meet Annie-Dot and her brother Joey."

"Hi," said Kit. Now she knew their names, but she still felt confused.

The ragged children waited expectantly while Jessamine opened her canvas sack and pulled out a chunk of bread. She passed half to each child. "Make it last if you can," she said. "And I have an apple, too. You'll have to share. That's all I could get today."

Then she pulled a library book from her bag and opened it.

"Read 'Little Orphan Annie'," begged the little boy, leaning close.

"You always want that poem, Joey!"

"It's a good one—but scary."

"Shh!" Jessamine cautioned. "Not so loud."

Kit sank to the ground and sat cross-legged amidst the fallen leaves, a million questions in her head.

"Read it in your creepy voice," begged Annie-Dot. "You do the best creepy voice!"

"You just love this poem because your name is Annie, too," Joey said.

"I don't know why you both like scary stories

so much," said Jessamine, shaking her head.

"It's 'cause we live *here*," said Joey, jerking his head toward the children's home. "Nothing is scarier than *here*."

"All right, all right." Jessamine lowered her voice dramatically and began to chant the poem. Annie-Dot recited along with her:

Little Orphant Annie's come to our house
to stay,
An' wash the cups an' saucers up, an' brush
the crumbs away,
An' shoo the chickens off the porch, an' dust
the hearth, an' sweep,
An' make the fire, an' bake the bread, an' earn
her board-an'-keep;
An' all us other childern, when the supper
things is done,
We set around the kitchen fire an' has the
mostest fun
A-list'nin' to the witch-tales that Annie tells
about,
An' the Gobble-uns 'at gits you

LITTLE ORPHAN ANNIE

Ef you
Don't
Watch
Out!

Joey squealed delightedly as his sister reached out and tickled him.

"More, more!"

"Shh!" hissed Jessamine.

Kit couldn't concentrate on the other stanzas. Why was Jessamine reading in secret? Why did the children need to be so quiet?

Now Jessamine's voice grew softer as she reached the last stanza:

An' little Orphant Annie says when the
blaze is blue,
An' the lamp-wick sputters, an' the wind
goes woo-oo!
An' you hear the crickets quit, an' the moon
is gray,
An' the lightnin'-bugs in dew is all squenched
away,—

*You better mind yer parents, an' yer teachers
     fond an' dear,*
*An' churish them that loves you, an' dry the
     orphant's tear,*
*An' he'p the pore an' needy ones that clusters
     all about,*
Er the Gobble-uns'll git you
Ef you
Don't
Watch
Out!

Again, Annie-Dot reached out goblin fingers and tickled her brother. But when their laughter rose delightedly, Jessamine said abruptly, "Enough! Hurry back inside before Matron notices you've been gone."

"Or we'll be sent to bed without dinner," said Annie-Dot. "I hate that."

"Yeah, but who cares? It's just mush, mush, and more mush," complained Joey.

"It's still food," Annie-Dot reproved him. "I'll take your serving *ef* you don't want it!"

"Shh!" warned Jessamine. "Run back—quickly!"

Joey reached out his hand. "Please can I borrow the book? I'll give it back next time."

"All right, but be careful!" Jessamine handed him the library book.

Whispering their thanks and waving goodbye, the children slipped away. From the cover of golden foliage Jessamine and Kit watched them sidle toward the building. They were just in time.

A pale, hatchet-faced woman in a high-necked black dress emerged onto the step. She raised her arm and rang a handbell to summon the children. They all came immediately to stand in two straight lines, one for the boys and one for the girls. The tension grew heavy as the woman stood frowning, clearly looking for any movement, listening for any voices. Then she rang her bell sharply, and the children marched in silence—boys through a door on the left and girls through a door on the right. Then they were gone.

As Kit and Jessamine walked back down

the hill, Kit was full of questions. "How do you know those kids? Why do you have to read in secret? I thought you lived there, too!"

Jessamine sighed. "Annie-Dot and Joey used to live next door to us. Their mother died last year, and their father left to look for work. He's supposed to pay money each month for their keep," Jessamine explained. "But he hasn't sent any for a long time. So they get very little to eat, and they have to work all day—well, all the kids do—scrubbing floors, doing laundry, washing dishes, mucking out stalls in the barn. It's hard work, and there's barely any playtime. I wanted to visit Annie-Dot, but only parents are allowed, and only once a month. And if you live in the orphanage, you're not allowed outside the fence. So one day I waited till they came out into the yard . . ."

She related how Annie-Dot and Joey had discovered the unlocked side gate and had started slipping out to spend their playtime with her in the grove. How they sometimes smuggled other friends out with them, and Jessamine brought library books to read to everybody. "They have hardly any books or toys," Jessamine said, "and there's no time, anyway, for playing."

"It sounds like a nightmare," murmured Kit.

The girls walked side by side, and Kit felt that it was almost like being friends with Jessamine again.

"Worst of all is Matron. She runs the place like a prison," Jessamine said. "I come every couple of days and bring extra food if I can, and more books. Annie-Dot is as hungry for books as for food. She especially loves mysteries."

"I can ask my friend Ruthie if we could borrow her Nancy Drew mysteries," Kit offered. "The kids could keep them for a couple weeks, to pass around."

"No." Jessamine shook her head. "They'd get in huge trouble. I shouldn't have given Joey that book, really. He could be punished."

"Punished—for having a *book*?" Kit couldn't believe it.

"Punished for everything," Jessamine said quietly. "For talking in the dining hall, or after lights-out. For crying when they're homesick. For being slow at their chores, or not knowing the answer at school. Their school is at the orphanage, too."

"Well, I'll get you the mysteries to read aloud to them." Kit paused. "So . . . what's your address? I'll bring you the books."

But Jessamine stopped at the corner and smiled lopsidedly. "I've got to go now. Goodbye, Kit." And she ran off, long legs flying, book bag thumping against her side.

Kit watched as she rounded the corner and was gone. *Foiled again,* she thought.

12

NO PLACE LIKE HOME

Kit felt a wave of gratitude when she saw the warm yellow light spilling from the windows of her house. How awful it would be to live in an orphanage like Goodmont. She wished some of the children could live with her. But she knew her mother would say they had enough mouths to feed in an overcrowded house.

As Kit walked around the house to the kitchen door, she found herself longing to talk to Ruthie about the children's home and the strange things happening at Rivermead. *The plain truth is, I miss Ruthie!* Kit thought. As she stepped into the warmth of the kitchen, she resolved to make up with her best friend the very next day.

But Kit didn't have to wait that long, because

Ruthie was sitting right there at the kitchen table with Mrs. Kittredge, stirring cubes of stale bread into a baking dish full of custard.

Kit ran over and gave her a hug. "Ruthie!"

"Oh, Kit! I've been waiting for you!"

"Ruthie's been a great help," Mrs. Kittredge said, sliding the baking dish into the oven. "We're making a quick bread pudding for dessert. She's been telling me all about the diary you found in her attic."

Ruthie's cheeks reddened. "The more I think about what I did, the sorrier I am. But I truly meant it all in *fun*. I felt terrible when I saw how disappointed you were."

"I can see why it would be upsetting to you, Kit," said Mrs. Kittredge. "But I also see very clearly that Ruthie meant it kindly, as a sort of adventure for you."

"I know that now," Kit said. "I'm sorry I was so angry." She hung her coat on the hook by the back door with her book bag. "I was going to tell you tomorrow at school that I'm tired of being mad."

Ruthie's eyes sparkled with relief. Kit felt as if a stone had rolled off her heart.

"You girls sit here and eat while you talk things out," Mrs. Kittredge told them. "And I'll be grateful if you'll watch that the bread pudding doesn't burn."

Kit and Ruthie helped serve in the dining room and then sat at the kitchen table to eat homemade noodles topped with chopped onions and cabbage from Kit's garden.

"I have *so* much to tell you," Kit said. "I can barely think where to begin."

"About Miss Mundis?"

"Yes—and orphans."

"Orphans?" asked Ruthie.

As they ate, Kit described the unhappy children and how Jessamine read to them secretly.

"I want to help," Ruthie said firmly, just as Kit had known she would. "But how?"

"Well, you have a big house. Maybe your family can take in all the children!"

Ruthie looked troubled. "Our house isn't

that big! But maybe Mother will donate food or clothing for the children."

"I know! I'll write an article about the orphanage," Kit said. "If people read about how badly the children are treated, maybe they will help."

Then Kit related all the strange things that were happening at Rivermead Manor and at Uncle Hendrick's house, too. By the time she'd finished, the bread pudding was ready to serve.

"No wonder you don't have time for fiction," Ruthie exclaimed as she helped dish up the dessert, putting two bowls aside for herself and Kit. "With all these real-life mysteries happening, who needs to make up stories?"

❧

After school the next day, Kit invited Ruthie and Stirling to come with her to Rivermead.

When they arrived at the iron gate, Ruthie's eyes grew wide as she stared at the manor house.

"Look at the size of this place!" said Stirling.

"How lovely to meet Kit's friends," cried Miss Mundis when she opened the door.

"You have a beautiful house," exclaimed Ruthie.

Stirling was bolder. "Kit tells us there's a secret room!"

"Yes," said Miss Mundis, "but I can't show you just now. Please do come in and have some hot chocolate."

Stirling's eyes lit up. Ruthie looked questioningly at Kit.

"Go ahead!" said Kit. "I still have work to do here and then at Uncle Hendrick's house, too. So why don't you two stay here and visit with Miss Mundis till I'm finished?"

"Good idea!" Stirling said. "I'll melt the chocolate."

"Just don't lick the spoon while it's in the pan!" warned Ruthie.

Kit dusted the parlor and swept the floors. Then she fried two eggs and made toast for Miss Mundis's supper. She drank a cup of cocoa herself while Miss Mundis sat with Ruthie and Stirling, showing them her magazines between bites of her supper.

"Thank you for leaving your friends with me," Miss Mundis said to Kit. "I'll look after them until you come back."

"Now tell us all about your time travelers," Ruthie urged their elderly host.

Kit headed out the kitchen door, reflecting on how happy and relaxed Miss Mundis seemed with her young guests. *She must often be lonely,* Kit realized. *It's so good to have friends!*

13

MYSTERIOUS UNCLE HENDRICK

Outside, Kit was surprised to see Uncle Hendrick in Miss Mundis's side garden, pruning the overgrown bushes near her back door. "Hello!" she called.

"You get to your work, and I'll be along soon," he told her, frowning.

Kit left him to his pruning, reflecting again that for a man who complained of arthritis, he was rather spry. Spry—but grumpy. *He needs cheering up,* she thought. She walked down Miss Mundis's sidewalk, through the gate, and along the street back to Uncle Hendrick's gate. After letting herself through it, she noticed the apple tree by the carriage house and decided to make him some applesauce from the last of the fruit hanging on its gnarled limbs. Homemade applesauce from her Aunt Millie's recipe never failed to please.

She clambered onto the low brick wall at the side of the carriage house and found that she was just able to reach the remaining apples. She was surprised there were so few left; last week the tree had been full of the red, ripe fruit. She plucked one apple and held up the bottom of her sweater to use as a basket to hold it before picking several more. Just as she was stretching to reach one last apple, she heard a door slam and felt a hand grab her wrist! Startled, Kit let out a shriek, and the apples in her sweater tumbled to the ground.

"Get down from there before you fall," a voice barked.

It was Uncle Hendrick! But where had he come from? There was a fence between Miss Mundis's yard and his. How had he gotten past her without her noticing? "How can you be here," she spluttered, "when I just saw you at Rivermead?"

Her great-uncle frowned at her. "Well, I came

home, obviously. You're here—and yet you were just there yourself. So why shouldn't I be here too?"

"Yes, but . . . so fast? How did you get here?"

"By spaceship, of course." Uncle Hendrick smirked. "Now, why are you picking apples when there are chores to be done?"

Kit knelt and gathered the fallen apples back into her sweater. "I'm making you some of Aunt Millie's applesauce." *To sweeten you up,* she added silently.

"You're not a bad kid, Kit," he said in a gruff voice.

Kit smiled at the unexpected praise and hurried back inside to peel and chop the apples. She set them on the stovetop in a pan of water, added sugar, and turned up the heat so that the apples would simmer. The apples would be ready to mash by the time she finished her chores and made Uncle Hendrick's supper.

While Kit was sweeping the stairs, Uncle Hendrick came inside. As she dusted the dining

room she could see him sitting at his rolltop
desk in the parlor.

She returned to the kitchen and mashed the
apples, adding a sprinkle of cinnamon. Then
she made cheese sandwiches. She found Uncle
Hendrick still at his desk, writing a letter. He
blotted the ink and then turned to her with his
usual look of impatience.

"Supper's ready," she said. "And I'm wondering if I may look in your attic for props for my
history project while you're eating. My friends
and I are putting on a play for our class."

"The attic?" He frowned. "There's only
old furniture up there. Too heavy to move for
playacting."

When her face fell, he added, grudgingly,
"There are a few trunks and boxes out in the
carriage house storeroom. Been there for years.
Organized just so. No rummaging!"

Kit went out to the carriage house and
climbed a narrow staircase to the storeroom.
Inside, crates and trunks held dishes and curtains and tasseled lamp shades. The air was

thick with dust. On a shelf by the window she spied some tarnished silver candlesticks. The candlesticks would work nicely for their skit, she thought. Kit reached for them but then stopped, her interest caught by an old trunk that stood open.

Unlike the other things in the storeroom, the trunk was free of dust. A frilly white petticoat trailed over the side.

Intrigued, Kit knelt in front of the trunk. Inside she found a tangle of long skirts and dresses and hats. Perfect costumes for their play!

"I told you not to go rummaging!"

She jumped at the sound of Uncle Hendrick's voice behind her and dropped the lacy petticoat.

"I'm not rummaging," she protested. "The trunk was already open."

"Don't you tell falsehoods, young lady," he snapped. "No one has been up here in years."

"But—look," said Kit. "There's no dust on this trunk. And it was already opened. This petticoat was hanging out."

"Nonsense. My mother's clothing was stored

neatly. What have you done with the rest of it?"

"Truly, Uncle Hendrick—this is just how I found the trunk. Only half full." Kit held up the petticoat, two skirts, and a feathered hat. "I'd like to borrow these, please. And these candlesticks."

He turned away, a frown creasing his forehead. "I thought I heard mice scratching up here the other day," he said. "But mice couldn't open a trunk and pull out the garments."

"It wasn't me, Uncle Hendrick, I promise." Kit shifted the things she was carrying so that she could cross her heart with her finger. "Cross my heart and hope to die!"

"There's no need for melodrama," he reproved her. "Still, you may borrow these if you return them promptly."

They went back to the house. Kit collected her book bag and coat, preparing to leave. Uncle Hendrick went to his desk in the parlor, folded the letter he'd been writing, and inserted it into an envelope. He opened a little pot of glue and brushed some on the flap to close it securely. "Your parents have told me that bothersome man, Mr. West, is boarding with you. Please give this note to him. I've written to say that if he pesters me again, my lawyer will file harassment charges."

Kit took the letter, but she hardly heard what Uncle Hendrick was saying. Instead, she stared at the handwriting—the firm, angular letters spelling out the name of Mr. Reginald West.

She had seen that writing before, very recently—on the scrap of paper from the secret room.

Kit ran back to Rivermead, the strangeness of this discovery making her heart beat fast. How could Uncle Hendrick's handwriting be the same as the writing on the old scrap of paper from the secret room? Could it be a trick—like Ruthie's trick with the diary? It was no secret that Uncle Hendrick didn't like Miss Mundis, but why would he want to trick her into thinking there were time travelers in her house?

Kit found Ruthie and Stirling in the parlor with Miss Mundis. Stirling was reading aloud from one of the *Amazing Stories* magazines. They all insisted that Kit wait till he finished reading it.

"Oh, that was a good one," Ruthie said breathlessly.

"Come again and we'll read some more!" Miss Mundis looked gleeful. "I'm happy to have company. It makes this old house feel alive."

On their way home in the gathering dusk, Kit showed her friends the candlesticks, the hat, the skirts, and the long petticoat. She told them how Uncle Hendrick had seemed to pop from the garden at Rivermead into his carriage house in an instant. And she showed them the letter for Mr. West. "It's the same handwriting," she said, comparing it to the scrap of paper she kept folded in her book bag.

"Definitely the same," said Stirling. "See the way he crosses his *T*s . . ."

"But the scrap of paper is old," Ruthie noted. "And the ink is faded."

"There are ways of faking that, aren't there?" Stirling asked pointedly.

Ruthie bit her lip.

"But why would he make a scrap of paper look old and somehow sneak it into the secret room?" demanded Kit. "*Why?*"

When they reached the road that led to the river path, Kit spied a familiar figure coming toward them up the hill, hurrying along with her head down.

"Jessamine!" Kit turned to Stirling and Ruthie. "I need to talk to her. Come on." Kit took off running. "Jessamine, wait up!" she called.

14
"THE PORE AND NEEDY ONES"

Kit ran after Jessamine, legs pumping hard, Ruthie and Stirling right behind. "Wait for us! We want to help!" Kit shouted.

Near the top of the hill, Jessamine whirled around. Her dark eyes flashed. "Stop following me! You'll spoil everything!"

"I'm sorry." Kit came to a halt. It took a few seconds to catch her breath. Stirling and Ruthie stopped, too, and Ruthie bent over, wrapping her arms around her middle.

"Why are you following me, Kit?"

"I told Ruthie and Stirling about how you've been reading to the children at the orphanage, and we want to help." Kit dug into her school-bag and handed Jessamine two Nancy Drew mysteries. "These are from Ruthie."

Jessamine accepted the books reluctantly. "Thanks."

"Did I see you in the garden at Rivermead the other day?" Kit asked her.

Without answering, Jessamine spun around and sped off like a rocket.

Kit, Stirling, and Ruthie watched as Jessamine reached the top of the hill and turned left. "I think she's heading back to the orphanage," Kit said, "and I want to go with her to help."

"Well, come on then," said Stirling. "What are we waiting for? We'll come with you. Right, Ruthie?"

"You bet!"

Up the hill they went, and there on the left was the high fence around the Goodmont estate. Children wandered in the bare yard.

"Crikey," said Stirling. "It's bigger than Rivermead!"

Kit beckoned them into the stand of trees. "Stay away from the fence, so nobody sees us."

They moved through the buckeye grove until

they found Jessamine. There were no children with her. Jessamine sighed audibly when she saw them. "You don't give up, do you, Kit?"

Kit looked around. "So where are they?" She kept her voice low.

"I don't know. It's the strangest thing," said Jessamine. "They always come! Annie and Joey sneak out as soon as they get yard time." She looked concerned. "They really should be here by now."

"Wait!" said Stirling. "Look there." He pointed to the fence. "Here comes a girl."

"That's Annie-Dot," said Kit.

Jessamine helped her through the rusty gate. "What's wrong?" asked Jessamine. "Where's Joey?"

"There's trouble," Annie-Dot said. Her eyes were red, as if she had been crying.

"Tell us," urged Kit.

"My brother is missing," wailed Annie-Dot. "No one has seen Joey since breakfast! He was caught reading the Orphant Annie poem instead of doing his chores. Matron threw the book on the fire and dragged Joey away. No lunch for him."

Her eyes were dark with worry. "I'm so sorry about your library book, Jess." She ran a thin, trembling hand through her curls. "But it was terrible for Joey. We all could hear him crying," she whispered. "No one has seen him for hours. Please help me look for him."

No one should be punished for reading a book! Kit thought as Jessamine slipped through the gate after Annie-Dot. Determined to help, Kit followed Jessamine. After a moment, Ruthie and Stirling came, too.

They had to approach the building without being seen. Some boys listlessly kicked a few balls around the yard, and a few girls crouched in the dirt playing marbles. "This way," Annie-Dot whispered. "It's closer."

She explained under her breath that this was the entrance to the girls' side. Kit saw narrow beds lined up in a long room. "The boys sleep in the left wing," Annie-Dot added. "And the babies are kept upstairs in the center section.

We're not allowed up there, though."

Kit wrinkled her nose. There was a sour smell inside the building, and the sharp odor of ammonia. She saw two tiny girls on hands and knees, scrubbing the floorboards.

"Why aren't they outside?" she whispered to Annie-Dot.

"Punishment for talking at lunchtime," Annie-Dot replied.

The children's home was quiet and bleak. "You'd think," Kit whispered to Ruthie, "with so many kids living here, there'd be laughter and talking. This is spooky."

"It smells bad, and there's a bad feeling, too," Ruthie said. "No wonder children are afraid here."

In every room they opened cupboards and looked under beds and tables. They checked the barrels of flour and oatmeal in the kitchen and the wooden washtubs in the laundry rooms. There was no sign of Joey.

"Someone's coming!" hissed Jessamine. They ducked into the shadows of the stairwell and held their breath while a man with a cloud of white hair and a bristly white beard clumped down the steps, whistling under his breath.

"That's Mr. McGregor," Annie-Dot said when he'd disappeared down the corridor. "He teaches the younger children. He's just about the only friendly grown-up here. Joey is so lucky! *My* teacher is as sour as Matron."

Kit shuddered and reached for Ruthie's hand.

"When Matron was scolding Joey for spilling his soup the other day, Mr. McGregor stopped her," Annie-Dot continued. She led them through the empty dining hall and paused at the stairs leading to the nursery. "The babies and toddlers are kept with a nursemaid," she whispered. "I hate to hear them crying so much. It's terribly sad. But you were so brave, Jess, sneaking upstairs that time, while the nursemaid was asleep—"

"Shh!" Jessamine cut Annie-Dot off. "We still have to search the outbuildings! Maybe Matron locked him in the old privy. Come on!"

They raced out the back door, crossing the

yard to check the outhouses. The bell rang, and children ran from all areas of the yard to line up in front of Matron.

"Oh—hurry," moaned Annie-Dot. "Into the barn!"

The barn smelled much better than the house, Kit thought. Two cows watched from their stalls. Chickens scratched in a pen.

"That's strange . . ." Annie-Dot looked around, frowning. "I gather eggs every morning, and usually that stall is open." She pointed at a stall in the corner of the barn. Now an iron bar with a piece of wood wedged through it bolted the door.

Kit crouched by the stall. "Hello?" She knocked on the wooden door.

She heard rustling sounds, and a small voice whispered, "Is that you, Annie?"

"It's Joey!" cried Annie-Dot.

Jessamine pressed against the door. "Joey, are you all right?"

"Yes! But I've been in here for hours and hours!" He added, his voice trembling, "It's so dark."

"Oh, Joey," wailed Annie.

Kit frowned. "We'll get you out," she vowed. She turned to the others. "This is awful. It must be against the law to lock children up."

"Happens all the time," Jessamine said grimly.

"Usually it's the basement," sniffed Annie-Dot. "That's where they put me when I dropped a sheet into the dirt while hanging laundry."

Kit and Ruthie stared at each other, horrified.

Jessamine tried to dislodge the wedge barring the door. Stirling tried next, but it held fast. Then Kit took a heavy hammer from the workbench and tapped hard on the wooden wedge. Would Matron hear the noise and come to investigate? Jessamine looked apprehensively over her shoulder.

Slowly, inch by inch, the wooden wedge slid out and finally dropped to the floor. Kit and Jessamine pulled open the door of the stall, and the little boy tumbled out. His tear-smudged face spoke of his ordeal. Kit looked into the small, bare space and tried to imagine being locked inside in darkness, with not even a blanket for comfort, and nothing at all to eat or drink.

"It's a risk, but we've got to give him water," said Jessamine. Using the pump at the side of the barn, she pumped a clear stream into a milk pail and brought it to Joey. He cupped his hands and drank thirstily.

"Now what?" asked Stirling.

"I won't go back!" Joey gasped, eyes blazing.

"Of course you mustn't go back," Kit said.

"We're going to run away," said Joey. "I made a plan while I was here." He turned to Jessamine. "You'll help me and Annie-Dot, won't you, Jess? Like you helped the others?"

The others? Kit stared thoughtfully at Jessamine.

And what was it Annie-Dot had said? *You were so brave, Jess, sneaking upstairs that time, while the nursemaid was asleep . . .*

Jessamine looked worried. "Where will you go?"

"To the hobo camp," said Joey. "Anywhere."

"It's not a bad idea," said Annie-Dot. "We've talked about it so often. They'll let us bed down for the night there, and in the morning we'll ride the rails out of this town. We can try to find our uncle who lives up in Cleveland."

Kit could only imagine how desperate she'd have to feel to leave everything familiar. But she saw very clearly that the orphanage was not a good place to live. Annie-Dot and her brother would do just as well, and maybe better, on their own, until they found their uncle.

They heard the crunch of footsteps on the gravel outside. Ruthie stared at Kit with panicked eyes.

"We have to hide!" hissed Jessamine. She put her arms around Joey and drew him close. "But where?"

Then Annie-Dot stepped boldly outside, squeezing her hands tightly together. *How brave*, Kit marveled, for surely she knew that punishment could follow. "Hello, Matron," said Annie-Dot. "I heard noises here and thought tramps were stealing the cows! You'll be glad to know the cows are all right."

"The cows are all right, are they?" It was Matron's voice, bitingly sarcastic. "All warm and snug, eh? And you came out to investigate?"

"I was coming to tell you, of course," said Annie-Dot brightly. "I thought maybe you'd want to alert the police."

Kit marveled at Annie-Dot's quick thinking, at the ease of her lies.

Desperate times call for desperate measures, Kit remembered. "This way!" she mouthed silently, pointing upward. "Quickly!" She pushed Ruthie toward the ladder of the hayloft, and Ruthie started climbing, with the others close on her heels. Like lightning, Kit grabbed up the wooden wedge from the floor and shoved it as hard as she could back into the bolt of the stall door. Then she fairly flew up the old ladder to the hayloft, where the others lay flat and silent on the wooden floorboards. Wisps of hay tickled Kit's nose as she stretched out next to Jessamine. *I mustn't sneeze*, she thought.

Through a wide space between floorboards, Kit could see Matron's form darkening the doorway. Matron peered inside the tack room. She glared at the locked stall.

An' the gobble-uns'll git you ef you don't watch out . . . Kit held her breath.

Behind Matron, Annie-Dot was silhouetted in the wide doorway of the barn, talking in a low murmur to another figure. And then Mr. McGregor appeared next to Matron. "This gal tells me," Mr. McGregor said in a raspy voice, "she thought there were thieves in here. D'you see anybody?"

"No," snapped Matron. "There's nobody here. Unless—" her eyes flicked to the ladder. "Unless they've hidden themselves in the hayloft."

Mr. McGregor stroked his white beard. "Well, I'd better check on that."

Kit's stomach lurched.

She heard him on the ladder and felt she might throw up. In a second his big, calloused hands gripped the top rung, and his grizzled head appeared. His kindly, watchful eyes met Kit's.

Please, her eyes implored him. *Please.*

He looked at Ruthie and Jessamine, whose eyes were squeezed tight, at Stirling huddled in the corner with his arms around Joey, as if to make them both invisible.

"No, ma'am," he called down to Matron. "Nothin' to see up here but some field mice. Now let's get Annie-Dot back to the house in time for some dinner. Perhaps she deserves an extra helping for tryin' to do a good deed."

Kit closed her eyes in gratitude and relief.

"Extra helping, indeed," sniffed Matron. "I don't know about that." But she left the barn, calling sharply to Annie-Dot, "Hurry up, girl! I've had enough of your nonsense."

Without saying another word, Mr. McGregor climbed down the ladder and left the barn.

It was a long time before the children felt safe to climb out of the hayloft. The cows lowed softly in their stalls.

Glancing around to be sure the coast was clear, the children slipped out of the barn and ran around to the side gate. They raced into the shelter of the buckeye grove.

"That was such a close call," said Kit. She was still shaking.

"Mr. McGregor saved my hide lots of times," Joey said, shivering. "Now which way is the hobo camp? I'd better run before Matron finds out I'm missing. I can wait there till Annie-Dot gets a chance to escape."

Stirling pointed down the hill. "Stay out of sight behind the trees as you go."

"Wait!" Jessamine twisted her hands together. "I'll take you, Joey. I know some people there who will help you till we can get Annie-Dot out."

"Wait," said Kit, digging in her schoolbag for a pencil. She tore a scrap off an old spelling test and wrote her name and address neatly on the back. She thrust it at Joey. "If Annie-Dot doesn't come, or you get separated somehow, be sure to write to your sister at my address.

Jessamine or I will take her the message."

Joey stuffed the scrap into his pocket. "Thanks," he said.

He and Jessamine started off down the hill. But Jessamine hesitated, turning back to Kit. "Thank you. Seems you helped us after all."

"Did you run away from here, too, Jessamine?" Kit asked urgently. "Please tell me. I'll keep your secret! Are you living in the hobo camp now?"

Jessamine shook her head. "I've never lived in an orphanage, Kit Kittredge! And I don't live in the hobo camp either. I live with my mama and daddy like you do. Just because my daddy isn't working for yours anymore doesn't mean we're homeless!"

"But why won't you tell me where you live?" cried Kit.

"I—I *can't* tell you." Jessamine stared at Kit. "Because . . . I promised not to."

The two girls faced each other. Kit searched Jessamine's face as if the answer would be found there.

Jessamine turned resolutely to Joey. "Let's go, then." She looked back at Kit and her friends. "Good-bye. Don't follow us this time. Promise you won't! Joey will be fine. People in the hobo camp will help him."

"We won't follow you," promised Ruthie.

"Wait!" cried a voice, and they all whirled around to find Annie-Dot coming toward them. "Wait for me!"

"You got away!" Joey hurled himself at his sister.

"When Matron sent me in to dinner, I told her that I needed to use the bathroom," Annie-Dot said, half laughing, half crying. "Then I ran outside and came straight here."

"We have to leave this very second," said Jessamine. "She'll be after you in no time."

Joey grabbed his sister's hand, and the three of them set off running. "Good-bye!" Annie-Dot called softly over her shoulder. "And thank you!"

Stirling called after them, "Good luck!"

Kit stood watching as they vanished down

the hill and into the dusk. *Escape!* It was a sweet word.

As they made their way home, Kit felt glad for Annie and Joey. But she couldn't help worrying about Jessamine. Jessamine didn't live at the orphanage, and she didn't live in the hobo camp, either. So where *did* she live?

Kit thought about the girl she had seen in the garden, and an idea took shape.

"Something's starting to make sense," she said to Ruthie and Stirling. "I think Jessamine's family became homeless after Mr. Porter lost his job. It's a pretty well-known fact that Rivermead has a secret room, so I bet they've taken shelter there."

"You mean *they're* the time travelers?" exclaimed Ruthie.

"But what about that bonnet you found?" demanded Stirling. "Why would they be wearing old-fashioned clothes?"

"Maybe they are so poor now, they don't have any clothes other than what they could find in the attic . . ." But Kit's voice trailed off, because Jessamine hadn't been wearing old-fashioned clothes, and the trunk of old clothes was in the carriage house at *Uncle Hendrick's* house, not Rivermead. How would Jessamine's family have gotten into Kit's great-uncle's carriage house to find those old clothes?

Kit bit her lip. "I don't see how all the pieces of this puzzle fit together," she admitted. "But I have a feeling Jessamine is somehow part of what's going on at Rivermead, and I'm going to look for answers tomorrow after school."

"We're coming with you," Ruthie promised.

15
OUT OF DARKNESS INTO LIGHT

Kit and Stirling had missed dinner, and Kit could tell that their parents had been worried. "Why did Uncle Hendrick keep you so long?" Kit's father asked.

"He didn't," Kit confessed as her mother bustled about the kitchen, warming bowls of vegetable soup and pouring glasses of milk. "You'll never guess who we ran into—Jessamine Porter!" She shot Stirling a warning look. It was best not to say anything just now about the frightening moments they had spent hiding at the orphanage. Kit was determined to find a way to help the unfortunate children there, and she might need to go back sometime. If her parents knew that she had been in danger from the matron, they might forbid her ever to return.

Quickly Kit changed the subject. "Uncle Hendrick gave me a letter for Mr. West. I'd better give it to him." She pulled it out of her book bag.

Mrs. Kittredge set two bowls on the kitchen table in front of Kit and Stirling. "You eat your supper, and I will take the letter to Mr. West. Though what business my uncle has with him is anyone's guess."

"It's to make Mr. West stop bothering him about opening his home to people who have lost theirs." And that reminded Kit of Jessamine. "Dad, do you remember Jessamine's father?"

"Certainly I remember Bert Porter." Mr. Kittredge nodded. "There wasn't an engine that man couldn't fix!"

"Well, do you know where he went after you closed your business?" Kit asked. "Because he must be living somewhere, but Jessamine won't say."

Mr. Kittredge raised his eyebrows. "I don't know," he said. "But a mechanic as good as Bert ought to find employment somewhere—that's what I told him."

"I hope so," Kit said, but she had her doubts. She and Stirling exchanged a look that said: *Maybe we'll know more tomorrow.*

After supper Kit did her homework. Then she brushed her teeth, put on her pajamas, and climbed into bed. She hoped that Annie-Dot and Joey had been given hot hobo stew for supper, and a warm blanket to cover them while they slept. The memory of the matron's cold eyes made Kit shiver. She pulled the covers up to her chin. It was wrong for such a person to be in charge of children, and it would be wrong for Kit to stay silent about what she'd seen that day.

When Mrs. Kittredge came to say good night, Kit clutched her mother's hand. "Oh, Mother," she burst out. "We visited the Goodmont Children's Home with Jessamine today, and it's a dreadful place!"

Mrs. Kittredge sat on the edge of Kit's bed. "Is it?" she asked.

"When we were there with Jessamine, we saw how the matron treats the children. She makes them work nearly all the time, and they say she punishes them all the time—for nothing! They're hungry and dirty, and—" Her eyes filled with tears. "Mother, can't we stop taking in boarders and bring orphans here instead?"

Kit's mother reached out a gentle hand and smoothed Kit's blonde bob. The touch made Kit's tears fall faster. "It's good of you to want to help children less fortunate than yourself. We'll report what you saw to the police, and they'll look into the situation. But we can't bring the children here, dear."

"Why not, Mother?"

Mrs. Kittredge stared out the window as if trying to see through the darkness of the Depression. "Because the children can't pay rent."

❧

Kit woke up that morning with a plan. She would write an article about the Goodmont Children's Home, describing the misery there. When people read the article in the newspaper, they would know that something had to change right away. She would urge them to bring children into their own homes to raise until their parents returned. She would urge orphanages to hire new staff—kind people like Mr. McGregor.

School passed in a blur. *The matron at the Goodmont Children's Home is cruel to the children in her care,"* Kit wrote furiously on the back of her spelling quiz. *The orphanage needs to hire staff who actually like children and will care about their welfare.* The ideas were coming thick and fast. She would describe how Joey had been locked in the stall. She would demand the matron's resignation.

After lunch the class worked on their projects. Stirling, Ruthie, and Kit practiced their skit. Ruthie and Kit wore the old-fashioned clothes Kit had found in Uncle Hendrick's carriage house. Stirling held a makeshift camera flash aloft and pretended to snap a photo. Kit, as the reporter, interviewed Ruthie as Harriet Beecher Stowe about how her work had influenced peoples' opinions about slavery. But Kit found it hard to remember her lines. All she could think of was Annie-Dot and Joey fleeing from Matron, racing toward freedom.

❧

After school the three friends hurried in the rain to Rivermead. Kit banged hard on the door, but no one came. Perhaps Miss Mundis was in the kitchen and couldn't hear because of the rising wind. Kit tried the door and found it unlocked.

Stepping inside, Kit called, "Hello, Miss Mundis!" But there was no reply.

"Where can she be?" Ruthie wondered.

Stirling said, "Maybe she's out in the garden."

"Not in this weather," objected Kit. She put out her hand for silence. "Shh! Listen!" She thought she had heard a faint cry coming from very far away.

There it was again! A cry like a kitten's. Was it Stanley? They followed the sound to the cellar door, which stood ajar.

The cellar light was on, but remembering the cellar's dark corners, Kit grabbed the flashlight from the pantry shelf anyway. They went down the steps, feeling the air grow cooler around them with each step, and followed the sound of the cry to the laundry room. The wooden panel that hid the secret room was open!

"Is that the hiding place?" asked Ruthie excitedly, crouching to see inside.

Stirling pushed forward. "Is Miss Mundis in there?"

Kit turned on her flashlight to illuminate the space. "It's empty," she said. "But I thought the cry came from here." Her beam of light fell upon a folded piece of paper on the floor against the far wall. She started into the room to get it.

Ruthie gasped. "Kit! Be careful!" She let out her breath in relief as Kit picked up the paper.

Stirling let out his breath, too. "You know, I was half expecting you to disappear into a different time!" Then he crawled after her into the room.

Ruthie followed. Kit trained her flashlight on

the paper. "What is it?" asked Stirling.

"It's got the same handwriting as on the scrap I found before. Uncle Hendrick's handwriting!" Kit read aloud:

". . . and desperate men have been known to do desperate things! I will wait until midnight. If you don't come, I will not trouble you again. But if you do—ah, the future will be ours."

Kit fished the scrap of paper from her book bag and held it along the torn edge of the larger paper.

and you have to realize how very desperate I have become—

"And desperate men have been known to do desperate things!" she read, and shivered, remembering that Mr. West had said nearly the same thing when he brought the chocolates.

Now they heard someone crying out again.

Impossibly, the sound seemed to be coming from the far wall.

"Miss Mundis?" Kit shouted. "Is that you? Where *are* you?" Handing Ruthie the flashlight, Kit ran her hands over the wooden planks in the end wall. She was searching for another knothole like the one that opened the secret room. And there, down low by the left-hand corner, her fingers found it. She pulled—and the wooden panel slid to the side. Kit had to press firmly so that the coiled spring wouldn't snap it back into place.

A tunnel yawned before them. Kit reached for the flashlight.

"Kit! What if it really *is* a time portal?" Ruthie asked, alarmed.

Stirling cautioned, "Careful, Kit . . ." He grabbed hold of the panel to hold it open.

Kit peered down the long, narrow passage as far as her light would reach. How would it feel to emerge at the other end of this space and be, after all, in a different time? Would it be the past? The future?

Putting such fanciful thoughts out of her head, Kit crouched low and stepped into the tunnel. She shone the light along the packed dirt floor. Ruthie and Stirling came right behind. All three gasped as the panel, released from Stirling's grip, sprang shut. Were they trapped?

"Help!" called a voice.

Miss Mundis!

The darkness seemed to pulse around the wavering beam of the flashlight. They had to bend low, and Kit felt as if she were walking through a thick dream fog. The tunnel must lead under the garden, under bushes, trees, and the crisp orange maple leaves that lay on the ground. It must be leading away from the house. But where did it end?

The air grew colder. There was a smell of damp earth. Kit's light wavered as it illuminated the old lady lying amidst a pile of rubble.

Kit knelt at Miss Mundis's side. "What happened to you?" she asked. Ruthie and Stirling crouched next to Kit.

"I've fallen again," cried Miss Mundis. "I'm so glad you children heard me!"

"But why are you down here?" Kit was relieved that Miss Mundis had tripped on the rubble; it had not fallen on top of her.

"Well, I was in the kitchen, and I heard a crashing noise! I came down to the secret room and heard more crashing in the tunnel. The water from the broken pipe must have seeped into the bricks and weakened the wall. I slid open the panel—but I had not brought a light, and when the panel door swung shut I was in darkness. I heard voices ahead of me, so I groped my way along, but then I tripped on these fallen bricks. Oh, I hope the time travelers have made it out safely . . ."

"Out where?" Kit asked. "Where does this tunnel go?"

"Hurry and see if they're all right!" cried Miss Mundis, clutching Kit's arm. "The tunnel may have caved in on them up ahead. Run all the way through!"

Stirling and Ruthie moved aside the fallen

rubble until they could proceed on through the tunnel. The path sloped gradually upward toward the tiny sliver of daylight they could make out at the end. But where was the end?

As Kit pushed against the metal grating at the end of the passage, she smelled the sharp odor of gasoline. A familiar voice thundered, "What in tarnation is going on here?"

Moving aside the grate, Kit began to climb out, and the first thing she saw was Uncle Hendrick's eyes, glaring down at her. He held a rag covered in automobile polish in his hand.

"Uncle Hendrick? What are *you* doing here?" Kit gasped.

Inky surged forward, yapping at Kit as she climbed the rest of the way out of the tunnel and looked around, blinking in the daylight. She felt like Alice in Wonderland down the rabbit hole, except that she had just come *up* from it. She realized she had seen the metal grate before, set low in the wall behind the parked automobile, but she had never given it a thought.

There was Uncle Hendrick's automobile, and

there was Uncle Hendrick, throwing his rag down and setting his fists on his hips.

"What am *I* doing here?" he thundered. "Why, I live here, Kit Kittredge! I'm polishing my motorcar. That's what I'm doing here! The question is, what are *you* doing here?"

"Miss Mundis is in there." Kit pointed back into the tunnel, from which Ruthie and Stirling were just emerging. "She's hurt."

Quick as a flash, Uncle Hendrick crouched down and entered the tunnel himself. Several moments passed before Kit saw Miss Mundis's silvery hair appear at the opening. Uncle Hendrick was behind her, supporting her. "Help pull her up, will you?" he ordered. He was frowning like a thundercloud.

With Kit on one side and Uncle Hendrick on the other, Miss Mundis limped to the motorcar and sat on the running board. "We must find them!" she cried.

"Find who, you crazy loon?" snapped Uncle Hendrick.

"The time travelers," Kit explained softly.

"Miss Mundis heard a crash from inside the tunnel, and she was worried that they were hurt. But they aren't in the tunnel, so that means . . ." She looked around the carriage house.

"Well, the carriage house was padlocked until I opened it," Uncle Hendrick said. "So whoever they are, if they came this way, they're still here."

The room fell silent, as if everyone were holding their breath. Then Kit walked cautiously around the automobile. She knelt down to peer under it. Nobody was hiding there. Then she headed for the tool room. The door was closed. She listened, and heard what sounded like a sob.

Slowly, Kit turned the doorknob. She opened the door. Inside, cowering under a workbench, were five pale-skinned children dressed in last-century clothing. Their red hair was tangled and matted. They were skinny and dirty, and they clung together like barnacles to a pier, sheltering from a stormy sea. They glared at Kit with bright, desperate eyes.

Miss Mundis's time travelers.

The two boys wore vests and long woolen trousers held up by suspenders. Two girls, younger than the boys, wore ankle-length skirts and shawls. The littlest girl, just a toddler, really, was bundled in a cornflower blue quilt. Kit recognized it from her bed at Rivermead. The little girl's curly hair was pulled into two small pigtails, one tied with a limp red ribbon. The other pigtail was missing its ribbon.

"We won't go back," the oldest boy, who looked about Kit's age, said defiantly.

"What in the world?" Uncle Hendrick's voice was gruff. "What are you doing here, you young scalawags?"

The oldest boy answered with a question of his own: "Have you seen our mother, sir?"

"Your *mother*? Why would your mother be in my garage, boy?" thundered Uncle Hendrick.

The oldest girl craned her neck, peering past Uncle Hendrick at the people crowding the doorway. "Is Jessie out there?" she piped. "Did she bring more food?"

"Who in tarnation is *Jessie*?" growled Uncle Hendrick.

Jessie! They meant Jessamine! Suddenly, things Kit had seen and heard at the orphanage made a different kind of sense. The five pale-skinned children looked a lot like the woman she had seen at the orphanage fence—and at Uncle Hendrick's back door the day she had met Miss Mundis. "You're Mrs. Addison's children," Kit cried. "The ones she left at the orphanage!" She turned to her uncle. "Remember, Mrs. Addison was looking for work—and she told us she had put her children into the orphanage? And then I heard that some children had run away— and no wonder, Uncle Hendrick, it's a dreadful place!" She turned to the children. "Jessamine Porter helped you escape, didn't she?"

The children glanced at one another, wordlessly communicating. Finally they nodded.

"She helped us get away, and she's been helping us ever since," said the oldest boy. "She comes most days—or whenever she can—to bring us food."

The oldest girl spoke up then. "Jessie's trying to help find our mother."

Uncle Hendrick opened his mouth, and Kit braced herself for his tirade against these intruders. Instead, he just motioned for them to leave the carriage house. "Come to the house," he said gruffly. "You all need something to eat."

"And hot baths," added Miss Mundis.

"I'll make sandwiches," said Kit. "If that's all right with you, Uncle Hendrick."

Kit held out a hand to the littlest girl, and after a moment's hesitation, the toddler put her hand in Kit's. Ruthie and Stirling took charge of the other children.

"We won't go back," the oldest boy muttered as they left the carriage house. "No matter what."

Uncle Hendrick offered Miss Mundis his arm and helped her walk to the house, Inky trotting along beside them. Inky swiftly claimed the loveseat in the parlor, but Uncle Hendrick nudged him off and settled Miss Mundis there instead. Then he sat next to Miss Mundis and examined her foot while the others gathered around them.

"First things first," Uncle Hendrick said. "I shall call for the doctor. This poor ankle of yours may be broken now, Elsie."

"Oh, you always did make such a fuss, Hen," Miss Mundis murmured. "Grumbling like a volcano about to erupt. But do call the doctor. I won't argue with you this time."

Kit listened with wide eyes.

They've known each other a long, long time, she realized. *And not only that—they like each other.*

She recalled the torn scraps of the old letter written in Uncle Hendrick's own handwriting. *I will wait until midnight . . .* Why would he have written that letter and left it in the secret tunnel—the tunnel that linked their two properties? She remembered the photo of Miss Mundis and a young man that she'd seen on her dresser. No wonder the man in the picture looked like her brother Charlie. It was Uncle Hendrick!

Kit marveled at the idea of these two old people, young then, leaving messages, visiting each other secretly. *They loved each other once!*

This new understanding made Kit laugh. "It was *you*, Uncle Hendrick!" she burst out. "You must have been the one who fixed that pipe!" And the lightbulbs—so conveniently appearing after Kit had told Uncle Hendrick about the troubles Miss Mundis was having at Rivermead Manor—could Uncle Hendrick have left those, too?

"You were sneaking through the tunnel and secretly helping Miss Mundis with repairs, and bringing her things. That's how you got back here so quickly after I saw you in her garden."

Miss Mundis chuckled and punched Uncle Hendrick lightly on the arm. "You sly dog," she said. "I should have guessed."

"Of course you should have." His smile at her was gentle. "I'm glad you see reason now."

"Reason? Oh, this is not to say that time travel doesn't exist! I'm quite certain it does. I just jumped to a conclusion prematurely in this case. But I'm pleased that my secret room was able to offer shelter again to people in need."

"And if any time travelers need to use it in the future, they are most welcome to," said Kit, grinning at Uncle Hendrick. "Right, Miss Mundis?"

"Load of nonsense," he grumbled. "Pair of Martians, both of you." He stood up. "I'm phoning the doctor before you fall any farther off your rockers."

He walked out of the room, and Inky raced after him, yapping at his heels. "Not now," Uncle Hendrick said. Inky jumped at the front door, still barking.

"All right, little fellow." He turned back and pointed to Kit. "Please take the dog out into the yard for a minute while I make the phone call."

Kit sighed and pulled open the heavy front door. *Trust Inky to be troublesome even in the middle of the most exciting events!*

Outside, darkness was falling. The air was crisp and cold. Inky ran to the bushes, still barking. He stopped short and braced his legs, pointing with his whole body.

"Shh!" hissed a voice from the bushes. A hand reached out and gave Inky a piece of bread. The dog took it and ran back to the front door, silent now.

"Who is it? Who's there?" called Kit. She blinked in surprise as Jessamine stepped from behind the bushes, holding her bulging book bag. "Jess!"

Jessamine looked equally astonished to see Kit. "You turn up everywhere, Kit Kittredge! I know you work at Rivermead. I didn't know you work here, too."

"I do," said Kit. "This is my uncle's house. Oh, Jessamine! I know what you've got in that book bag. It's food, isn't it?"

Jessamine hugged the bag to her chest. "Why—why would I have food in my bag?"

Kit shook her head. "Come on, Jess. There are five kids wearing old-time clothing inside the house who were asking for you by name! They're runaways from the children's home, as I think you know perfectly well. They said you helped them escape, just like you helped

Annie-Dot and Joey. And you brought them here to hide!"

"So you found them!" Jessamine nodded slowly. "Oh, Kit, I know it was wrong to let them hide here, but the kids were so desperate. Their father had gone to New York to look for work. And their mother had nowhere for them to live. They couldn't manage with their baby sister in the hobo camp, so I had to find them somewhere else to live until their mom came back. I was just coming to bring them some bread, but they weren't at our usual meeting place. I was worried!"

"How did you meet them in the first place?" asked Kit.

"Annie-Dot brought them to me. Maggie and Weezy, and Eddie and Horace—they're all great kids, and they were all so worried about their little sister, Baby Bev. She was kept in the nursery, and Matron wouldn't let them see her! When they tried, she punished them. So I helped them make a plan."

Jessamine held up her bulging schoolbag.

"I always gather up whatever extra food I can find," she said. "My mother makes me a sandwich for my lunch every day, but I always put half aside and save it for the other kids."

"So that's why I saw you in this neighborhood. You were coming to Rivermead to help these kids. They've been here all this time."

Jessamine sighed, and her shoulders slumped. "I'm not sorry the children have been found out. It's been a big responsibility looking after them all."

"Well, come in," urged Kit. "Everybody else will want to hear your story."

Kit brought Jessamine into the parlor, and the Addison children jumped up and ran to her. As she told her story, they chimed in.

Jessamine had learned at school that Rivermead Manor had a secret cellar room where slaves used to hide. She had discovered that the outside cellar door at Rivermead was unlocked. She thought the room might be a safe place for the children to live while they searched for their mother.

OUT OF DARKNESS INTO LIGHT

Once they'd rescued Baby Bev from the nursery, they met in the grove and slipped away in the middle of the night. They'd pulled open the outside cellar door and crept into Rivermead Manor while Miss Mundis was sleeping. "Jess knew about the secret room because she'd read about it in a book," said the girl named Weezy. "But then we found the secret passage all by ourselves."

"We explored the carriage house, too," the other girl, Maggie, admitted. "We found warm clothes in the old trunk. I know it wasn't right to take them, and I know we look silly, but they've kept us nice and warm."

Weezy had watched Baby Bev during the day while the others searched for their mother and foraged for food. When Uncle Hendrick's house was open and Uncle Hendrick was busy with his automobile, she had sometimes slipped inside his house, too. "Sorry about taking the sandwich and the milk," muttered Weezy. "We were just so hungry . . ."

"We didn't mean to steal," Eddie added

earnestly. "And we tried to make up for it by bringing flowers."

"We also borrowed some magazines to read," Horace confessed. "They were great! And we found some old papers in a cigar box in the tunnel, but they were just mushy love letters."

Kit reached into her pocket and pulled out the torn scraps. She handed them to Uncle Hendrick. "These probably came from that box. They belong to you, I think."

His cheeks reddened. "What—?" he sputtered. "They're nothing."

Miss Mundis took them and read them silently. Her cheeks grew pink. "Actually they're very precious indeed." She reached out a hand, and after a long moment, Uncle Hendrick held it tightly.

Miss Mundis smiled. "Let me tell you a story," she said. And while they waited for the doctor to arrive, she told how, when she and Uncle Hendrick were teenagers, many long years ago, they had sneaked back and forth through the secret passage to visit each other because her strict Victorian parents refused to let her keep company with boys. When he was a young man, Uncle Hendrick had asked Miss Mundis to marry him. "We met out by the apple tree," she said. "And he got down on one knee and asked if I would become his wife."

"But she turned me down," said Uncle Hendrick, and he released Miss Mundis's hand. "Turned me down flat."

"I just couldn't marry without my parents' blessing," Miss Mundis said softly.

"I figured you had some other lad in mind." Uncle Hendrick looked away. "I figured there was no point in hoping or waiting."

"And you barely spoke to me ever again!" Miss Mundis swatted his arm. "Too proud to ask me to marry you even after my parents died years later. And I was too ladylike to ask you myself."

Kit knew the end of this story. Over the years, Uncle Hendrick had shut himself away from people, growing grumpy and reclusive, while Miss Mundis lived alone in her big house just next door, taking solace in her science fiction.

"But when you heard Miss Mundis was hurt, you wanted to help," Kit exclaimed. "You went secretly through the tunnel. So you still like her!"

"You're a sharp girl, Kit," said Uncle Hendrick. "You get that from my side of the family."

"Well, the question now," said Miss Mundis, "is what to do with these homeless waifs. And I have a very good solution in mind." She smiled at the Addison children. "You must live with me! And when your mother is found, if she would like a job as my housekeeper, she can help with the boarding house I mean to start running. Once we have some boarders, I'll have the money to pay her. Mr. West was right, I think. There are so many people needing help these days, we must all rise to the occasion if we can." At Kit's exclamation of delight, Miss Mundis smiled. "Having you and your friends in the house, Kit, has shown me how much I enjoy having young ones around."

The doctor arrived then, and he wrapped Miss Mundis's ankle, which was not broken but badly sprained. Then Uncle Hendrick drove Miss Mundis the short distance to the gate at Rivermead, while the five children walked over. After everyone helped Miss Mundis get settled on the sofa with a cup of tea, Uncle Hendrick said, "I'll be back shortly, Elsie, to help with all your time travelers. But first I must drive these other meddlesome creatures home." He nodded toward Kit, Stirling, and Ruthie.

Kit smiled. She thought of all the times he must have crawled through that grate and gone back and forth to Miss Mundis's house, and of the way he had practically lifted Miss Mundis out of the tunnel. *So much for his arthritis,* she thought. *I think mostly he was suffering from loneliness.*

"You too, young lady," he called to Jessamine. "I'll drive you as well."

"*If,*" added Kit, "you'll tell us where you live, Jessamine."

Jessamine sighed as she followed them into

the car. "It wasn't meant to be a mystery. It's just that where I live is supposed to be *secret*." She turned to look at Kit. "It's not that I don't want to be friends, Kit. I do!"

"Where to?" Uncle Hendrick asked as he started the car.

Jessamine directed him along the streets to a school. "Stop here, please," she said.

Kit looked at the school building and back at Jessamine in surprise. "You live at your school?"

"Not exactly," said Jessamine. "But my father is the boilerman, and my mother mops the floors. They're so grateful to have employment, but we didn't have any place to live after we lost our house. Then Dad discovered an empty storage shed at the back of the school property. It's tiny, but better than nothing. Still . . . it's not really ours. We're just *borrowing* it. Secretly."

She opened the car door and thanked Uncle Hendrick for the ride. Then she turned to Kit. "And now I've broken my promise, but I hope you won't tell. Maybe someday your father will have his business back, and we can sit in the automobiles and go on our pretend journeys again."

"And swing in the tree," added Kit, her heart feeling light. "We won't tell anyone, Jessamine."

Ruthie was dropped off next. Kit and Stirling arrived home just in time to take their usual places at the dinner table. Uncle Hendrick was invited to join them, but he declined, telling Mrs. Kittredge there were people waiting for him. "Young mouths to feed," he said. "You know how it is!"

Kit's mother stared after him as he tipped his hat and left the house. "How strange," she said to Kit. "Do you know what he's talking about?"

"As a matter of fact, I do," said Kit. She looked around the table at all the boarders. "And it's quite a story."

❧

Alone in her bedroom, Kit rolled a new sheet of paper into her typewriter. How to begin her article?

She thought of Miss Mundis and Uncle Hendrick, who had a chance for a new friendship now, and of Jessamine, who still wanted to be friends with her. She thought of Annie and Joey, out in the world on their own, and of the Addisons, who would find work and a home at Rivermead, and of the many children still at the orphanage. She thought of the way her article would help make things better for them.

She typed her headline:

TIME TRAVELERS UNMASKED:
Frightened Runaways from Children's Home Find Shelter on Underground Railroad

We're all time travelers of a sort, Kit thought. *Just traveling through our own lifetimes, trying to make the best of things . . .*

Her fingers tapped the keys.

LOOKING BACK

A PEEK INTO THE PAST

The Cincinnati home of Harriet Beecher Stowe. In 1852, she wrote Uncle Tom's Cabin, *a powerful novel against slavery. In Kit's time, an excellent school for black children was named for her.*

In Ohio, where Kit's story takes place, slavery had been against the law since the state was established in 1802. But in states south of Ohio, slavery was legal until the 1860s. Because Kit's hometown of Cincinnati was just across the river from slave states, many men, women, and children fleeing slavery passed through the city on their way to freedom in northern states and Canada.

Free states are shown in orange, slave states in green.

As they made the dangerous journey north, escaping slaves often found shelter, food, and other kinds of help on the *Underground Railroad,* a kind of informal support network run by both blacks and whites who opposed slavery. Histories of the Underground Railroad often mention secret rooms and tunnels where escaping slaves could hide, although no one knows if a secret passage like the one in the story actually existed in Cincinnati.

Enslaved people faced great risks as they escaped to freedom. People who helped fugitives on the Underground Railroad put

Top: A tunnel in an Ohio house rumored to have been used by escaping slaves
Below: A man running from slave catchers

This museum display shows a cutaway view of a house on the Underground Railroad, revealing its secret hiding places.

their own safety at risk as well, because it was illegal to help an enslaved person escape. So it's very unlikely that a real girl whose family helped fleeing slaves would have written about it in her diary, as Ruthie wanted Kit to believe in this story.

By the time Kit was growing up in the 1930s, slavery had been illegal in America for more than 70 years. But black Americans still did not have full equality under the law. Businesses could legally refuse to hire workers simply because

Frances Scroggins Brown, one of many black Cincinnatians who helped slaves escape on the Underground Railroad

they were black—so, as hard as it was for white workers like Kit's dad to find jobs during the Depression, it was far more difficult for black workers to find jobs. In addition, landlords could refuse to rent to black people, and public places such as schools could require blacks to remain separate from whites. Even some charities, like soup

A poster from the 1930s advertising separate swimming lessons for white and black children

kitchens, refused to serve black people. For all these reasons, the Great Depression, which made life brutally hard for many white families, was even worse for black families like Jessamine's.

The Great Depression was especially hard on children, too. American orphanages had always taken in children whose parents had died and

Soup kitchens served food to the hungry during the Depression.

Thanksgiving in an orphanage, 1933

also so-called "half orphans"—children whose parents were living but not able to care for them. During the hard times of the Depression, orphanages grew more and more crowded. Like the fictional Goodmont Children's Home, they could be wretched places to live. Children in orphanages often had to earn their keep by working, and they might be punished for breaking even minor rules. Parents sometimes had to pay the orphanage to care for their children; if they couldn't pay, the children might be put up for adoption. It's not surprising that some children tried to escape, as the Addison children do in this story. Not all orphanages were terrible places, however. Many were run by dedicated people who tried hard to provide a good home for the children in their care.

It's no wonder that during the depths of the Depression, people were often desperate for anything that would take their minds off how difficult life was. During Kit's time, science fiction stories like the ones Miss Mundis enjoys were printed in inexpensive publications called "pulp magazines."

Science fiction magazines from Kit's time

Stories were also broadcast on the radio, a very popular form of entertainment at the time. In 1938, radio stations broadcast one of the most famous science fiction stories ever— a frightening tale called "War of the Worlds," in which Martians invade Earth. The broadcast was based on the novel of the same name by H.G. Wells, which had been written many years earlier. But science fiction was still not very well

A recording of the science-fiction radio broadcast that terrified the nation in 1938

known, and the radio drama was presented as breaking news, interrupting regular programming. So people across the country believed that the radio drama was real—and they were terrified!

Generally, though, fantastic stories of time travel and flying cars offered an escape from the hard times of the Depression. They may also have offered hope: their vision of the future was one in which new inventions could solve serious problems, and marvelous experiences were just around the corner.

A science fiction illustration that Kit might have seen

About the Author

Kathryn Reiss lives in a rambling 19th-century house in northern California, where she is always hoping to discover a secret room or time portal. Ms. Reiss's previous novels of suspense have won many awards. When not working on a new book, she teaches creative writing at Mills College and enjoys spending time with her family.